February 2004

To Paul,

with best wishes,

from Maryellen

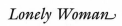

Lonely Woman

Weatherhead Books on Asia
Columbia University

LITERATURE

David Der-wei Wang, Editor

Ye Zhaoyan, *Nanjing 1937: A Love Story*, translated by Michael Berry

Makoto Oda, *The Breaking Jewel*, translated by Donald Keene

Han Shaogong, *A Dictionary of Maqiao*, translated by Julia Lovell

HISTORY, SOCIETY, AND CULTURE

Carol Gluck, Editor

Lonely Woman

Takahashi Takako

introduced and translated by Maryellen Toman Mori

Columbia University Press   New York

Columbia University Press wishes to express its appreciation for assistance given by the Weatherhead East Asian Institute Publications Program toward the costs of publishing this book.

Columbia University Press
Publishers Since 1893
New York   Chichester, West Sussex

Library of Congress Cataloging-in-Publication Data
Takahashi, Takako, 1932–
    [Ronrii ūman. English]
    Lonely woman / Takahashi Takako ; introduced and translated
by Maryellen Toman Mori.
        p.   cm. — (Weatherhead books on Asia)
    Includes bibliographical references.
    ISBN 0–231–13126–7 (cloth)
    I. Mori, Maryellen Toman.   II. Title.   III. Series.
PL862.A42146R613   2004
895.6'35—dc21   2003053205

Columbia University Press books are printed on permanent and durable acid-free paper.
Printed in the United States of America
c 10 9 8 7 6 5 4 3 2 1

Contents

Translator's Acknowledgments

Several institutions and individuals provided me with support while I was engaged in this project. A National Endowment for the Humanities Summer Stipend enabled me to devote myself to preliminary work on the translation during the summer of 1997. The Northeast Asia Council of the Association for Asian Studies funded a trip to Kyoto in September of that year to conduct a series of discussions with Takahashi Takako. A fellowship from the Japan Society for the Promotion of Science allowed me the rare luxury of a lengthy sojourn in Kyoto in 1999. The International Research Center for Japanese Studies hosted my stay during that time. The tranquil environment of the center facilitated my concentration on this and other scholarly undertakings. Santa Clara University granted me a leave of absence in 1999 to take advantage of the opportunity to spend the year in Japan.

I wish to sincerely thank Takahashi Takako for giving me the privilege of translating her literature, and for generously sharing her time with me during our several memorable visits in Kyoto. Warm thanks are due to Leslie Kriesel at Columbia University Press for her careful editing of the manuscript. I am grateful to Martha Evans, former Director of Book Publications at the Modern Language Association, for her longtime encouragement of this project. Paul G. Crowley, S.J., former director of the Catholic Studies Program at Santa Clara University, took an interest in my work on Takahashi and gave me an opportunity to present my research to other members of the program. Cynthia Bradley, library specialist at Santa Clara University, good-naturedly persisted in locating sometimes-obscure materials by and about Takahashi for me. Naomi Kotake, Japanese book cataloger at Stanford University's East Asian Collection, kindly helped me track down various pieces of bibliographical information. Special thanks go to my son, Jonathan Masami Mori, whose sweetness and good humor renew me, and to my husband, Shōzō Mori, whose love and support have sustained me over the years.

Introduction

Takahashi Takako: A Biographical Sketch

> When she surrendered to desire, a passionate woman emerged from deep within her. A woman far more intense than her usual self, a kind of madwoman—open, impetuous, lusty, vibrant, as focused as a murderer. An unfamiliar woman, yet one whom she felt she'd known from before she was born. If she were to ask, "Who are you?" that woman would surely reply, "I am you. . . ." (*Wasteland,* 406)

Female characters in Takahashi Takako's fiction often engage in scandalous behavior to actualize latent aspects of themselves that are more daring than their ordinary social personae. According to the author, the process of creating such defiant fictional characters has a similarly liberating effect on her. Contrary to what the above quotation might suggest, Takahashi's writing typically gives an impression of cool rationality that is rare in Japanese literature, especially by women authors. Japanese critics have praised her meticulously crafted novels for their formal perfection and restrained, lucid prose, and have attempted to analyze their philosophical premises. But despite her obvious intellectual inclinations, for Takahashi, the main significance of fiction writing lies in its effectiveness as a mode of exorcising personal demons and of nurturing unborn "selves" to which she aspires. Madwomen, murderers, nymphomaniacs, painters, musicians, mystics—the passionate, often dramatically antisocial characters that inhabit her fictional world—are dormant alter egos that she discovers by delving deep into her "inner ocean," as she often calls the subconscious mind, and "scooping them up." Her unruly fictional characters bear little outward resemblance to their creator, whose lifestyle has been unusually sequestered and austere. In this sense, too, her literature goes against the grain of modern Japanese belletristic writing, which, in accordance with a long tradition of fusing fiction and autobiography, often adheres quite closely to the contours of its author's actual life.

Takahashi (Okamoto) Takako was born in Kyoto, Japan, in 1932, the only child of well-to-do, cultured parents.[1] To this day, when she is in Kyoto she stays in her spacious childhood home, which was designed by her father, an architect. It is located in a placid old neighborhood near the famous Kinkaku (Golden Pavilion) Temple.

As the ancient capital of Japan and the cradle of a culture fostered by aristocrats at an imperial court, Kyoto takes pride in its noble heritage. The city continues to conserve traditional aesthetic and social values, including deference to male superiority and authority. While acknowledging the profound influence of her native place on shaping her psyche and personality, Takahashi has often expressed her aversion to certain aspects of Kyoto's distinctive culture. In an essay entitled "The Kyoto Woman Within Me," she compares the traditional Kyoto woman to a snail, deeply withdrawn into its shell, which never exposes its innermost self to the outside world. She attributes this trait to the deep-rooted, oppressively patriarchal environment of Kyoto, which conditions women to constantly suppress their own thoughts and feelings and maintain a bland, compliant demeanor, so that the men in their lives can exercise their wills without encountering resistance. Writing became a way for Takahashi to develop and assert her individuality and express her desires and illicit impulses.

Takahashi attended Kyoto University, one of Japan's most distinguished academic institutions, a rare accomplishment for a woman of her day. There she majored in French, writing her senior thesis on Charles Baudelaire and graduating in 1954. Later that year she married Takahashi Kazumi, a fellow graduate who had earned his degree in Chinese literature. An aspiring writer, Kazumi soon quit his night school teaching job to devote his spare time to fiction writing, while continuing his study of Chinese literature in graduate school. For several years, Takako worked at various jobs—secretary in a small factory, translator, tutor, and tour guide—to support them both. She idolized her husband for his brilliance, literary talents, and exquisite looks. An idealistic intellectual, she had no interest in material comforts, nor any desire for children or ordinary family life. She just wanted Kazumi to become a successful writer, and she devoted considerable energy to helping him realize this dream. But she managed to preserve her own literary interests as well; in 1956 she returned to Kyoto University to pursue a master's degree in French literature, which she completed two years later, with a thesis on François Mauriac.

From 1958 to 1965 the couple lived in an apartment in a suburb of Osaka. Takako's privileged background made her ill prepared for life in a typical middle-class apartment complex. She did not share the conventional values and desires of the housewives there, and she despised the conformity and tedium of community life. She found it awkward to associate with the "ordinary" people who surrounded her at home and at work, and she resented the frequent intrusions by friends and acquaintances upon her and Kazumi's private world. In

1961, her sense of alienation and ennui prompted her to begin writing her own novel, *A Ruined Landscape*. She would later recall her plunge into fiction writing as a desperate attempt to "save" herself by creating an artificial world, convinced that "beauty springs from a denial of everyday reality" ("Reflections on My Maiden Work," 167).

In 1962 Kazumi's novel *Hi no utsuwa* (*Vessel of Sorrow*) won a major literary prize, and he was thereby established as a writer. The substantial cash award enabled Takako to quit her various jobs and devote more time to her own literary activities. She began writing short stories, continued working on her novel, and published a Japanese translation of Mauriac's novel, *Thérèse Desqueyroux*. At the same time, she became busier than ever helping Kazumi in his career, providing him with clerical and editorial assistance and waiting on his many houseguests. Kazumi's increased involvement in the local literary scene made Takako acutely aware of the exclusive, male chauvinistic nature of the literary establishment in the Kansai region of Japan.[2] After he received the prize, Kazumi's circle of literary acquaintances and his sphere of career-related activity greatly widened. This, however, did not benefit Takako, socially or professionally. Kazumi shielded his wife from the public eye, as was customary. It went without question that she would not accompany him to the literary events and gatherings that he was constantly attending. When her husband's friends or fellow literati came to visit him at home, Takako had to behave according to her socially defined role as a wife; she would serve the men tea, but not participate in their conversations. The rare woman who held strong opinions was expected to refrain from voicing them, regardless of her intellectual abilities or educational background.

Takako began to yearn to leave the Kansai area. In 1964 she became a member of a Tokyo-based literary coterie in whose magazine, *Hakubyō*, she published her first short stories the following year. In 1965 Kazumi accepted a teaching position at Meiji University in Tokyo and the couple moved to Kamakura, a quiet, historic city not far from Tokyo. The main reason for the move was so that Kazumi, whose career was flourishing, could be near the hub of literary activity in Japan. Takako felt greatly relieved to be away from Kyoto and within range of the more progressive atmosphere of Tokyo. Little by little, her work began to benefit from the contacts she made among Tokyo literati, whom she found more receptive to professional women than their Kansai counterparts. When Kazumi accepted an offer of an assistant professorship in Chinese literature at Kyoto University, beginning in 1967, Takako refused to return to Kyoto with him. For the next two years she flouted convention by living alone, apart from her husband, in order to devote herself to writing and developing her career. She published many stories and essays during this time. Kazumi would join his wife in Kamakura during his university holidays, but in Takako's heart, their relationship had changed irrevocably. She knew that she could never relinquish her newfound independence and artistic recognition for a life of subordination and self-effacement.[3]

In 1969, just as Takako's literary career had begun to bear fruit in the form of numerous publications, Kazumi, who had always been physically delicate, began having serious health problems and returned to Kamakura to be with her. Shortly thereafter he was diagnosed with cancer. Takako nursed him devotedly until his death in 1971.

The 1970s was a decade of tremendous intellectual and social expansion, literary activity, and professional success for Takahashi. Generally speaking, Japanese women's literature, which after centuries of oblivion had gradually been reappearing since the late nineteenth century, burgeoned. During this era, most female authors of serious fiction sought to express feminist consciousness and concerns by means of a wide range of realistic and experimental literary techniques. The *Zeitgeist* was propitious for literary women like Takahashi who were talented, ambitious, and eager to reconfigure traditional female images and roles. Takahashi published prolifically in several genres—short stories, novels, essays, a memoir, and translations of French literature. Her first two short story anthologies contained mostly macabre tales of "mad housewives" and other dangerous or deranged women, written in a surrealistic vein. These collections were enthusiastically received in literary circles. Takahashi soon came to be identified with a cluster of distinguished writers (such as Furui Yoshikichi and Mori Makiko), labeled "the introverted generation," who wrote dark, introspective works. By the end of the decade she had published four highly praised novels and eight short story collections; three of these works won major literary prizes. An astute literary critic herself, Takahashi was in demand as a book reviewer, and as an essayist and a participant in dialogues and discussions on literary topics.

In 1974 she began regularly attending talks on Christianity. Her interest in the religion had been piqued by her reading of European literature at university, and later, of novels by François Mauriac, Julien Green, and others. The ordeals and upheavals in her personal life over the previous few years prompted her to learn more, and the subtle infusion of Christian symbolism into her literature was beginning to effectively unify her fictional world and enhance its distinctiveness. In 1975 she spent a week at a Carmelite convent in Hokkaidō, and shortly thereafter she was baptized a Catholic.

Even after she had reached a pinnacle of professional success, Takahashi was still plagued by discontent and a sense of unease in Japanese society. Since her husband's death, she had often traveled to France and found the atmosphere there refreshing and congenial. In 1980 she went to France imagining that she would never return to live in Japan. She has written that her lifelong sense of oppression lifted when she began living there ("Passing Through the 'Dark Night,'" 536). While in France she devoted herself to practicing the pipe organ. (She had begun learning to play the instrument in 1978, having developed a great fondness for Bach chorales during previous trips to Europe.) She also became deeply involved in the religious life of a Catholic contemplative association that had been established in Paris in 1975 by a charismatic French priest. She began writing essays on religious topics in Japanese and publishing them in Japanese magazines, and eventually in books. She also continued writing and publishing fiction in Japanese. From this time on the theme of spiritual quest became central to her fiction, some of which is set in France. After 1982, as she became more seriously involved in religious practices, she wrote fiction only during her biannual trips to Japan to visit her parents. In 1985 she published the novel *Child of Wrath*, which is set in Kyoto and written in Kyoto dialect. Critically acclaimed as a masterpiece, the novel won the prestigious Yomiuri Prize the following year. Takahashi wrote the work to deal, at last, on an artistic level, with her deeply ambivalent feelings toward her native place.[4] She intended to crown her fiction writing career with this novel, and afterward to devote herself entirely to spiritual pursuits. In 1985 she became a nun in the religious society to which she belonged. But as this organization expanded and evolved, it became embroiled in financial difficulties and power struggles. In 1988 various deceptions and improprieties perpetrated by members of the group began to surface, and Takahashi felt compelled to quit it.[5] She returned to Japan, and in 1989 she entered a Carmelite convent. She remained there only a year, as she found its rigidly hierarchical structure too confining for her. In 1990 she moved to her family home in Kyoto to care for her elderly mother. (Over the next ten years her mother grew progressively senile, eventually becoming totally dependent on her.) Since returning to Japan Takahashi has continued to write prolifically in an array of genres—essays on both secular and religious topics, memoirs, translations of French Christian writings, a biography, a trilogy of works (a novel, an essay collection, and a play) linked by spiritual themes, and a trilogy of novels loosely based on her experiences in France.

Takahashi Takako's Fictional World

Nihilism and Misogyny

From her youth, Takahashi was attracted to late nineteenth- and early twentieth-century French literature—the poetry of Verlaine and Mallarmé, the novels of Proust and Gide, and later, to fantastic fiction, surrealist literature, and Christian literature. The motif of journeying to exotic lands or escaping into an imaginary or supernatural dimension struck a resonant chord in her. In a 1994 essay she remarks that for her, the appeal of these diverse writings lay in their common theme of "the rejection of the things of this world and the flight to other realms." She continues, "I suppose I chose Baudelaire as the topic of my senior thesis in the Literature Department because I responded deeply to this recurrent motif in his poetry. Although I wasn't fully conscious of it at the time, in retrospect I see that in youth one's soul intuitively discovers its lifelong theme" ("This World as a 'Wasteland,'" 553–54).

Besides identifying with Baudelaire's world-weariness, his yearning for transcendence, and his fascination with evil, Takahashi imbibed the rampant misogyny and antinaturalism in his writings. All these tendencies color her own early works, in which western decadent values are infused into a purely Japanese milieu. In her texts, most women are portrayed as contented, earthbound creatures who are incapable of metaphysical aspirations, in contrast to a nihilistic, rather narcissistic female protagonist who withdraws from contemporary reality in pursuit of a private utopian realm.

Many of Takahashi's early short stories depict a morbidly sensitive female protagonist who feels alienated from patriarchal society's definitions of femininity and trapped in a body and a lifestyle that she experiences as restrictive and demeaning. She is repelled by her female relatives and acquaintances and by what she perceives as the vulgarity and triviality of their lives. "Captive," for example, portrays a single woman in her early twenties who feels revolted and suffocated by the women who surround her, all of whom embody some negative stereotype of femininity. Her older sister, with whom she lives, is a frustrated, neurotic married woman. Their next-door neighbor is a hefty, jovial middle-aged woman who wears sheer pink underpants and fishnet stockings and serves her guests large slices of sickeningly sweet cake. That woman's mother is a witchlike crone who walks around muttering hexes and making dire pronouncements. Even superficially amiable female relationships are tainted by an undercurrent of petty rivalries and jealousies, nosiness, deceptions, and vindictiveness. The delicate heroine, for whom marriage and motherhood have no appeal, longs only to escape from the loathsome morass of female associations in which she feels helplessly mired, and to re-create herself in different terms. But she has no means of self-definition or path of escape, except in her imagination. She asserts her difference from the women around her by indulging in fantasies of pushing each of them downstairs to her death.

The protagonist of "Yonder Sound of Water" is a married woman living in a drab housing project who suffers from a similar sensation of claustrophobia and irritation. She entertains murderous fantasies toward her own daughter, a constant odious reminder of her own female biology, social role, and certain unattractive personality traits. One day, as she gazes at a photograph of herself as a girl, she seems to hear a distant sound of clear, running water. Later, on a group outing, she escapes alone into a forest. Here she has a nostalgic, hallucinatory encounter with a girl, the spirit of her childhood self, who personifies her lost youthful purity and beauty. In the above stories and others, the heroine's rejection of normative adult female selfhood is enmeshed with her desire to forge an alternative identity or reclaim a prior one. She dreads the prospect of being engulfed by a community that squelches deviation from its norms and values women only for their procreative function and maternal qualities.

In "Yonder Sound of Water" Takahashi invokes the *dopplegänger* (double) motif, an obsessive theme in her fiction, in both its positive and negative aspects. Other stories, in which the double is a wholly repugnant figure, feature a woman whose tenuous personal boundaries are threatened by a daughter, sister, or female acquaintance. This woman violates the protagonist's sense of integrity by resembling her to an uncomfortable degree, seeking intimacy with her, or reading her mind. In many of these stories, the heroine is overwhelmed by resentment toward what she perceives as a parasitical simulacrum and fantasizes killing her, or actually kills her, in order to regain her sense of identity. In a few stories, a female double arouses an ambivalent response in the heroine, who is torn between desires for both privacy and intimacy. In "Symbiotic Space," for example, the heroine takes comfort in the uncanny telepathic connection that she shares with her sister, in contrast to the emotional distance between her and her husband. At the same time, she wishes to erect barriers against her sister's prescience, experiencing it as invasive.

Although negative portraits of female relationships dominate the literature produced by Takahashi in the first half of her career, even among her earliest stories one finds prototypical representations of women who are drawn to other women as figures of wisdom, compassion, or guidance. Such positive relationships play a significant role in some of her later works. In these stories, however, the affirmation of female bonds is not predicated on a feminist vision of solidarity based on a shared experience of gender-based discrimination. It suggests, rather, the expanded possibilities for relationship available to those engaged in a fundamentally religious process of dismantling the individual, gendered self. Takahashi's early literature reflects the initial stage of this process through its depictions of female protagonists who reject mainstream models of subjectivity, especially as personified in traditional Japanese womanhood. Her later works represent the phase in which this process is consciously undertaken and has begun to bear fruit; they include female (as well as male) characters who enjoy relative freedom from gender-related restrictions or who relate to others in transgendered terms.

Many of Takahashi's texts may be interpreted as female narratives of awakening, in which a woman's quests for erotic fulfillment and spiritual understanding are inextricably entwined. But because of its many unusual features, her literature eludes easy generic classification in terms of modern Japanese literary history. Her nearly exclusive focus on a protagonist's interior landscape, her extensive use of a fantastic narrative mode and decadent-aesthetic motifs, and her incorporation of Christian symbolism and themes are rooted in a personal visionary perspective that distinguishes her work from that of her contemporaries. This complex combination of traits renders her literature at once broader and more idiosyncratic than would allow it to be subsumed under such categories as feminist, psychological, or ideological fiction, much less the native Japanese "I-novel," which is fashioned from the raw materials of the author's daily life.

Crime, Madness, Desire, and the "Lonely Woman"

Takahashi's texts depict the "lonely woman" not, fundamentally, as a pathetic figure but as an extraordinary one, by virtue of her keen self-consciousness. Often she perceives herself as special and resists assimilation into community life in order to savor the sensation of herself as a unique individual. Takahashi's fiction affirms the woman who engages in antisocial behavior as a person who has awakened to her inner self and is asserting it in defiance of conventional norms. Criminals and madwomen are two versions of the ubiquitous "lonely woman" archetype in her works. Takahashi views the criminal who acts alone as a "spiritual adventurer"; by renouncing the comfort of companionship and experiencing the thrill of transgression in solitude, she confirms her self-reliance and sharpens her awareness of human isolation ("A Literature of Murder," 15–16). The author is also intrigued by madness as a symptom of unfulfilled sexual desire. She believes that women are more prone to this condition than men, as women are far more sexually restrained, by nature and by social mores ("'Going Mad,'" 204–5). Her stories depict madwomen as individuals who have an exceptional capacity and need for exhilaration and who will to go to any length to try to obtain it. Takahashi romanticizes such aberrant people, discerning enormous vitality in their drastic behavior, however irrational or immoral it is by bourgeois standards.

Takahashi's glorification of the female outlaw is partly indebted to surrealist philosophy and literature, of which she was an avid reader. Like the surrealists, Takahashi valorizes crime, madness, and *"amour fou"* as forms of rebellion against repressive social forces that liberate libidinous energy and thereby enrich one's sensibility. The protagonists of Takahashi's first three novels are all women who behave cruelly toward individuals who have done virtually nothing to deserve their enmity. *To the End of the Sky* depicts a woman who brings about the deaths of her husband and child in a fire, simply because she cannot endure their constant close proximity to her. Later, she is irritated by a friend's gentle disposition, which she senses is somewhat insincere; this mild, semiconscious irritation escalates into lethal hatred that drives her to kidnap the woman's baby, and then to mistreat the child. *The Tempter* portrays a cynical university student with an interest in demonology who encourages two friends to commit suicide by jumping into a volcano crater. *A Ruined Landscape* features a troubled woman who is drawn to a Catholic nun with a pious air. When she suspects that the nun has a hidden wanton side she feels betrayed, and sets about to humiliate and destroy her. Infuriated by the meek, the smug, and the commonplace, and hungry for knowledge, power, and sublime experiences, these characters feel a profound discontent that manifests itself in sadistic behavior or gratuitous acts of violence.

Lonely Woman is Takahashi's most sustained and multifaceted fictional realization of her concept of "loneliness." The collection occupies a pivotal position in her *oeuvre*; it continues the exploration of illicit desire that characterizes her prior works, and it ends with a story revolving around renunciation of worldly attachments, a theme whose religious nuances become increasingly evident in her subsequent literature. There is a feminist aspect to *Lonely Woman*, since the "loneliness" that plagues the female protagonists of the stories is on one level related to their sense of social alienation as women who deviate from conventional norms of feminine feeling and behavior. However, these women evince no self-pity over their solitary existence or yearning for the diversions of ordinary social life or the solace of community. Their fidelity to an inner voice compels them to act in accordance with its promptings. They surrender to their passionate impulses, risking psychosis and social opprobrium, as if instinctively attempting to tap into the creative and spiritual reservoir at the heart of their taboo desires. In "Why I Became a Catholic," an essay written in the same year (1977) that *Lonely Woman* was published, the author reflects on her proclivity for depicting "lonely" individuals:

> Critics often complain that I portray only introverted characters. Apparently this means characters who are withdrawn into madness or delusion, and who make no attempt to communicate with others. Some have commented that the characters I create are people who are incapable of loving others. . . . I want to make it clear here that I intentionally depict such characters. . . . Because every human being has a place that he can't communicate, and that others have no way of knowing; this ultimate solitude that all humans endure is, I think, the key point of human existence. . . . Moreover, I've come to think that it is in the depths of a person's soul, the place that another person has no way of knowing, that God reveals Himself. (187–8)

Takahashi strongly identifies with the anguished characters in the novels of François Mauriac, whom she calls "incarnations of insane passion" ("*The Desert of Love* and God," 46). Like Mauriac's Thérèse

Desqueyroux, Takahashi's female characters are proud, intelligent, chronically dissatisfied women who vent their frustration on relatively innocent targets. Takahashi's entire fictional *oeuvre* is primarily an exploration of desire—"thirst," as the author usually calls it. Vexed by the inadequacy of everyone and everything they encounter, her restless, intense heroines are driven to extreme behavior by their insatiable desire for something more. In her fictional world, as in Mauriac's, this thirst, which heightens their potential for both rapture and destruction, contains the seeds of spiritual awakening. As the nun in *A Ruined Landscape* says to the distraught protagonist who abuses her: "Inside you is a huge hollow, and along with that, or rather, because of it, is raging thirst. Cherish your thirst, your desire to fill up that hollow with something. . . . Because you thirst, God exists" (67).

A religious vision is adumbrated even in Takahashi's earliest literature. Crime and illicit passion are not merely protests against conventional morality and social and gender norms but also signifiers of a nameless craving that has no earthly object. Takahashi's typical female protagonist's rejection of quotidian reality and quest for something ineffable at times seems to signify her narcissistic wish to merge with that ineffable force and become a self-sustaining world. Be that as it may, in Takahashi's texts crime is portrayed as a path some individuals must follow in order to quell their diffuse rage and induce a shift in their perspective. Through violence, such a person simultaneously discovers her capacity for destruction and her limits as a human; this realization stimulates in her a dim apprehension of a luminous realm. The target of her violence is cast as a sacrificial victim who is an unwitting catalyst of the protagonist's awakening, or in Christian terms, an instrument of grace.

Heterosexual Love

Takahashi writes that since her youth she had long believed that the only thing of value in life was unconventional love between a man and a woman ("This World as a 'Wasteland,'" 537). Throughout her fiction, a woman's pursuit of rapturous erotic experience is a recurrent theme. Often erotic transport is closely linked to psychic integration, mystical illumination, aesthetic pleasure, or a combination of these. *Wasteland*, *The Heavenly Lake*, *The Lost Picture*, and other novels, as well as a host of short stories, describe relationships in which women use men as conduits to a heightened state of consciousness. Through ecstatic sexual activity, often of a somewhat deviant nature, the women awaken to a source of inner power or experience a sensation of release from mundane reality.

The female protagonist of *Wasteland* seeks gratification with numerous partners, including her sister's husband and near strangers, with no regard for the practical consequences. Through her reckless behavior, she tries to discover and release a kind of primitive female energy that she senses within herself. She regards men as channels for contacting this "inner woman," vaguely realizing that it is she, rather than her male partners, with whom she is truly in love. Other stories focus on the relationship between a middle-aged woman and a very young man, whose delicate, androgynous beauty is a fusion of aesthetic perfection and sacredness. Even if there is no carnal relationship between the two, there are strong erotic overtones, usually incestuous in nature. Although the perverse scenarios described in these texts often seem on the surface to be the epitome of decadence, devoid of ideological nuances, they arguably have feminist implications. An assertive older woman enacts her fantasy of a gender role reversal in her relationship with a feminine, docile young man, thereby subverting her culture's dominant gender paradigm. Takahashi's lovingly detailed descriptions of such ethereal, doll-like, amoral youths are found in many of her works, and these images, together with their implications, constitute one of her literature's most beautiful, if disturbing, aspects.

In *The Heavenly Lake*, for example, a forty-two-year-old female artist has as her lover and model a languid, compliant, exquisitely beautiful youth who is half her age. His name, Tamaki, connotes a gemlike, perfect circle. The woman delights in drawing him in nude poses that emphasize his "feminine" vulnerability and suggest that he has been raped. Her artistic purpose is to evoke "the feminine element that is discernible neither in an adult male or female nude, but only in the body of a young man" (54). She enjoys the youth as an object of aesthetic and erotic pleasure and a creature that yields to her wishes. At the same time, because of his aura of purity, poise, and remoteness, she idealizes and worships him, realizing that she can never possess his elusive spirit. In other stories, such as "Doll Love" or *The House of Rebirth*, the boy is so ethereal that the reader is not sure if he is supposed to be real or a hallucination conjured up by the female protagonist's yearning. Sometimes the beautiful boy is depicted as a woman's muse, or as an angelic figure who comprises both sexes and has sensual as well as spiritual qualities.

The Unconscious

Takahashi is endlessly fascinated by the concept of the psychic unconscious, and her understanding of it is obviously indebted to western psychoanalytical models. Her preoccupation with the notion of a divided self and her interest in its diverse literary representations are reflected in her essays on literature. Among these are discussions of numerous western classic fantastic tales, such as Honore de Balzac's *Séraphita*, Edgar Allan Poe's "William Wilson," Oscar Wilde's *The Picture of Dorian Gray*, and E. T. A. Hoffmann's "The Sandman."[6] Many of Takahashi's own works represent a conflict between the conscious and unconscious levels of the mind by invoking the motif of doubles or by portraying an individual who is torn between opposing desires or senses that she exists simultaneously in two dimensions of reality. For instance, various stories involve a character whose amiable social persona masks murderous drives, or who is alternately in the grip of sadistic and masochistic impulses, or who cannot distinguish between fantasy and reality.

The theme of the split self is sometimes expressed through the motif of spiritual twins or an individual who is androgynous or bisexual. Dreams play a vital role throughout Takahashi's literature. Some of her female characters escape into dreams or fantasies as a desirable alternative to everyday reality. Others, like the protagonist of "The Oracle," are obsessed with their dreams as a source of truth.

The unconscious is represented positively in some texts, as a repository of energy or beneficial occult knowledge to which only a fortunate few are able to gain access. In others it is depicted as a foul quagmire harboring destructive urges that may erupt on provocation, with catastrophic results. Some of Takahashi's female characters are terrified of succumbing to irrational impulses and losing control of themselves. Others pursue visionary consciousness by actively attempting to tap their dormant psychic potential through strange rituals of their own devising. In *The House of Rebirth*, for example, a woman in her forties and her teenage lover engage in various mildly sadomasochistic rites. They aim to strip off their respective social personae and recover from the dark "well" of the collective unconscious an impersonal, "archetypal" relationship that the woman believes they previously shared. Female characters in many of Takahashi's stories seek self-obliteration through violent or ecstatic experience in order to escape, even fleetingly, their painful sense of self-division. Throughout Takahashi's *oeuvre*, scenes representing the blissful shattering of personal boundaries form a counterpoint to those that portray women fending off invasive influences in order to consolidate their subjectivity.

Takahashi often uses water imagery as a metaphor for the psychic unconscious. In *The Tempter*, for example, the protagonist, a nihilistic young intellectual, senses a dark, menacing ocean within herself that she constantly struggles to suppress. She leads two female friends to their deaths, although she harbors no conscious hostility toward them. She vaguely senses that she is in the grip of an "unknown self," and she feels disconcerted by the violent impulses that bubble up from deep within her. In *Child of Wrath*, a more affirmative work, ocean imagery serves a similar function. The protagonist, Mioko, is a sensual, intuitive young woman who is susceptible to disturbing dreams and premonitions that she is unable to analyze or express. She sometimes feels in danger of losing her fragile sense of identity and being carried away on a turbid, churning ocean of anxieties and desires. At these times, the shining waves that seem to emanate from her cousin, a devout Christian woman whom she admires and trusts, temporarily subdue Mioko's inner chaos and prevent her from being overwhelmed by it and swept away.

The Religious Dimension of Takahashi's Literature

Takahashi's continually evolving understanding of Christianity is highly personal and unorthodox, and thus she has remained on the periphery of Japan's small cohort of so-called "Christian writers." Her early interest in Christianity was entwined with her rather morbid taste for tales of devils, doubles, and supernatural occurrences in European literature. Later, after she became a Catholic, it was the writings of mystics such as Simone Weil, St. Teresa of Avila, and St. John of the Cross, along with esoteric Christian meditation practices, that she found compelling, rather than the doctrinal and mainstream devotional aspects of the religion. During her lengthy residency in France, she intensively studied Christian mystical literature in French and engaged in contemplative practices based on those described. Since then, her interpretation of Christian mythology seems to have broadened to not only transcend sectarian distinctions but also blur the marks that would bind it to any particular religious tradition. In fact, this expansive, border-crossing tendency has always been reflected in her fictional works that are ostensibly imbued with Christian themes; this is partly attributable to their fusion of disparate cultural elements. In her story "As I Walk Through the Endless Valley of Woe," for example, the protagonist's sense of individual identity, along with her suffering

over a man's infidelity, dissolve in a vision of the interconnected-
ness of all beings. This perspective resembles the Buddhist concept
of enlightenment as a realization of the delusory nature of the ego.
And *Child of Wrath*, although delicately tinged with Christian symbolism, was lauded by Japanese critics mainly for its impeccable
rendering of the psychology, speech, and interpersonal dynamics of
Kyoto people. In a published interview with the author, a well-
known Japanese literary critic (Akiyama Shun) gently expressed
skepticism that this novel's underlying mentality was consistent
with a Christian worldview. His consternation arose from the
work's portrayal of murder as a natural and inevitable result of the
protagonist's rage over unrequited love and female malice. The author responded: "The God of love exists eternally, behind and beyond all human phenomena. All human events take place within
the sustaining embrace of that loving gaze. This is what Christians
believe, and viewed in this way, murder and God are not incom-
patible" (*Child of Wrath*, "Supplement," 9).

From her early explorations of female fury and frenzied desire, in
which religious nuances are so muted as to be imperceptible to the
casual reader, to her most recent, in which a woman's pursuit of
spiritual understanding is highlighted, Takahashi has instilled Christian symbolism into her fiction with great subtlety. In this respect
she differs from her friend and mentor, the late Endō Shūsaku, who
is the best known of Japan's Christian authors. Endō's earthy,
parable-like stories often subordinate aesthetic considerations to an
evangelical agenda, and his aim to attract a large readership contrasts
sharply with Takahashi's indifference to popular appeal.

Takahashi's treatment of the spiritual quest theme becomes
more prominent in her literature written after 1980. In her early fiction, unconventional heterosexual love is represented as a woman's
main path of self-realization. But in her later works, erotic love is
depicted as a hindrance to spiritual development, simply a form of
carnal pleasure, or at most, a pale version of the love between

human and God. She has written that she now views mystical illumination, a state that is achieved in solitude, as a purified form of eros ("Passing Through the 'Dark Night,'" 548–51). In any case, most of her stories written after 1980 depict women who, to varying degrees, renounce sensual love for spiritual pursuits. This shift away from the portrayal of heterosexual erotic love as a vehicle of emancipation is accompanied by a much more positive treatment of female nature, female relationships, and women's capacity for growth independent of male intermediaries. This reconfiguration of thematic emphases is evident in *Child of Wrath*, *Prepare Thyself, My Soul*,[7] and "Ceaseless Encounters." The short story "To Love," recipient of the 1985 Kawabata Prize, is noteworthy for its portrait of a mature, independent woman, happily involved in a relationship with a rather ordinary man, who has achieved a certain balance in her life between sexual love and love of God.

The publication of *Exile* in 1995 marked Takahashi's return to fiction writing after a decade in which her literature, mainly in the form of essays, was devoted entirely to religious subjects. Set in France, the novel concerns a Japanese woman writer on a spiritual pilgrimage who meets a married couple with whom she is deeply impressed. She begins writing a novel that she calls *Exile*, modeling the main characters on that couple. The two love each other, but they live apart for long periods of time in order to devote themselves to contemplation. At some point, the man is inspired to change his name from Daniel to Marie-Daniel. He does so partly in homage to an eccentric Benedictine monk who is devoted to the mother of Jesus and who goes by the name of "Brother Marie." Daniel develops a close bond with this man and also regards him as a spiritual mentor. Toward the end of both the protagonist's novel and the one that frames it, Marie-Daniel leaves home to lead an ascetic life alone in the desert, "where nothing exists but God's joy" (278). While he is away, his wife discovers and reads a journal entitled *Exile* that her husband was keeping. At the end of the journal Marie-Daniel describes a vision that he has had of walking through the desert and seeing the entire dry landscape within himself. Suddenly a narrow canal full of blue water, extending through the desert, appears beside him. Then the white desert sand becomes transparent, and the ocean that lies beneath the earth rises and floods the entire desert. He keeps walking, the boundary between the external world and his inner world having completely dissolved. Marie-Daniel seems to embody Takahashi's ideal of an individual whose mind has expanded to encompass the world, with all its illusory polarities. The author later wrote of her attraction to and identification with this character: "As soon as I began writing *Exile*, a Frenchman named Marie-Daniel emerged from within me, and I was transformed into him for the entire time I was writing the work. Indeed, it is his life that I am still living" ("France, My Love," 174).

Lonely Woman: *The Stories*

The short story collection *Lonely Woman* consists of five individually titled short stories that are linked by certain characters, themes, and plot elements. Takahashi wrote the stories intermittently, publishing them in various literary journals between 1974 and 1977. The collected stories were published in book form in 1977, and that year the work was awarded Japan's sixteenth annual Women's Literature Prize. Japanese critics praised *Lonely Woman* for its crisp prose and the dramatic, plot-driven nature of its stories. They especially admired the author's orchestration of the individual works into a cohesive whole through her skillful handling of a seldom-attempted form, the linked-story sequence. The work's careful design no doubt accounts for those aspects that some readers perceived as slight weaknesses; they contended that its conceptual underpinnings cause some incidents to seem contrived and certain characters a bit stereotypical. Critics' interpretations of the unifying theme of "loneliness" varied somewhat. Some understood it as the madness lurking just beneath the surface of

the lives and psyches of apparently normal individuals who are socially isolated. Others read it as a condition afflicting women of the
1970s, an era in which the women's liberation movement, among
other forces of social transformation, presented them with new
freedoms and choices that caused some to become mentally unstable. Matsumoto Tōru's analysis is particularly astute, shaped as it is
by his familiarity with Takahashi's earlier fiction, his close reading
of this work, and his sensitivity to the author's sensibilities. He observes that female characters in all the stories "are carried to the
brink of self-destruction by something that emerges from within
their loneliness, but at that point these women become more fully
alive" (216). He discerns similar significance in the author's pen-
chant for solitude: "Whereas most contemporary people are tormented by inner poverty, as a result of her self-imposed, extreme
isolation, Mrs. Takahashi suffers from inner plenitude" (217).

Takahashi was writing the stories that comprise *Lonely Woman*
during roughly the same time frame in which she was writing *The
Tempter*, her most relentlessly nihilistic work. *Lonely Woman*, too, is
a dark work overall, mainly because of the futile yearning that
plagues most of its female characters. But the work's atmosphere is
saved from bleakness by the author's wry humor, the diverse cast of
colorfully drawn characters, and the brief flashes of beauty and
pleasure that brighten some of the female characters' otherwise
dreary lives. The last story, "Strange Bonds," focuses on an elderly
woman who has attained a measure of self-acceptance and equa-
nimity. It incorporates several of the characters who appeared in the
preceding stories, viewing them from the detached perspective of
the protagonist. The story thus serves as a lens through which the
reader may reinterpret the previous ones. The final scene of this
story casts a poignant glow over the whole collection.

In her essay "Sexuality: The Demonic and the Maternal in
Women," Takahashi writes, "I suppose that when a woman truly lib-
erates the female within her, a demon appears. . . . Any woman who

through some circumstance awakens to her inner self is a demonic woman, and I suspect that the majority of women, who are unenlightened, are merely suppressing their demonic tendencies" (87–88). By "demon," she seems to imply a form of primal energy that cannot be completely subdued or extinguished by the socialization process. Each of the stories in this collection can be read as a variation on the theme of a woman awakening to an "other" within her.

Sakiko, the protagonist of "Lonely Woman," is a woman in her late twenties who lives alone and works at a job in which she has long since lost interest. Her cynicism and ennui are conveyed to the reader through her contemptuous attitude toward and caricature-like perception of the people around her: the sensible housewives in her neighborhood; a garrulous spinster who makes unsettling predictions; an earnest, rather simple-minded policeman; a good-natured male co-worker whom she tantalizes.

Sakiko's deviance from dominant gender norms is indicated by her unmarried status and her aversion to children. When there is a series of arsons at local elementary schools, she repeatedly imagines "countless young children shrieking, roasting to a crisp in that inferno with no exit." Her misanthropy extends to men who are attracted to her unconventional manner and takes the form of sadistic manipulation. When she makes a date, instead of meeting the man, she conceals herself and observes him from a distance. She finds it much more enjoyable to watch a man grow irritated as he waits for her than to keep company with him.

Sakiko's curiosity is aroused when she hears of the arsonist. She supposes that the culprit is not a vicious individual, but a bored, intelligent, alienated woman like herself, who has the audacity to act out her hostile fantasies on a grander scale than Sakiko. When she reads a newspaper article about "lonely women" in London, she is similarly excited by its description of solitary women who stand out in a crowd. Such women appear to bear a brandlike mark of their extraordinary nature and to emit "a peculiar blend of decay and vigor."

Sakiko's identification with the arsonist intensifies until she begins imagining that she herself set the fires. She is seized by an impulse to confess to the deeds and be recognized as the criminal, and thereby to fully liberate the lawless woman she senses lurking within her.

Yōko, the protagonist of "The Oracle," is a naïve, childlike woman who becomes extremely sensitive to subliminal messages. Disturbing dreams about her dead husband and other women, including her sister-in-law, whom she had trusted and admired, convince Yōko that her "model husband" was unfaithful to her. "Beautiful things always conceal an underside that is anything but beautiful," she muses. As she grows increasingly prone to regarding people's social personae as mere masks that they wear to hide their improper desires or shameful behavior, an analogous inversion occurs within her; her dream life becomes more real than her actual life and threatens to dominate her consciousness completely.

Yōko's range of feelings and behavior are expanded as a result of this unnerving infiltration of subconscious material into her waking life. As her dormant memories of the distant past awaken, she recalls the mortification she experienced in high school when a boyfriend rejected her in favor of a female classmate. Her long-repressed anger over this incident surfaces and incites her to perform an uncharacteristically aggressive action at the story's end. "Soon I won't be having those dreams anymore," she reflects with grim satisfaction. For Yōko, avenging her past victimization through a vodoulike rite is a way of venting her rage at female treachery and male infidelity, whether real or imagined. At the same time, by pacifying her fury in this manner, she apparently hopes to drive similar troubling thoughts into her subconscious and prevent them from making further intrusions into her awareness.

Ichiko, the protagonist of "Foxfire," has a tedious job as a department store clerk. She suffers from a chronic malaise that she attributes to the tendency in Japanese society to squelch individual differences. At times, "every single cell in her head felt heavy. It was as if the cells were encrusted with sticky soot, and no matter how much she slept, she couldn't free herself from that sensation." Ichiko is revitalized by her encounters with mischievous children. One day at work she witnesses a girl deftly steal a wig and some frilly underpants, and afterward act seductively with a male doctor who is called to examine her. When Ichiko escorts the girl home, she enjoys a rare, lighthearted mood; simply being near the brazen child temporarily releases her from the feelings of oppression and intimidation that normally beset her while walking in a crowd. At the same time, her feelings toward the girl contain "something akin to the dread that a slug or a lizard inspires." She encounters several other children whose naughty or precocious behavior suggests the presence of something wild or sinister inside them: a child who keeps emitting a birdlike shriek in a supermarket, a group of children who rip up a patch of daffodils and dash off, a little boy who flirts with her in a train. The vicarious thrill that Ichiko obtains from her encounters with these impish youngsters hints at her secret longing to shed her inhibitions and indulge in some misbehavior herself.

For Haruyo, the protagonist of "The Suspended Bridge," it is passionate erotic love that stimulates the emergence of dormant facets of her personality. When she learns that a suave, elusive man with whom she had had a torrid affair in college is living in the same city as she, her passion is awakened for the first time in many years. As she reminiscences about the emotional extremes that she experienced during her relationship with this man, Igawa, her placid domestic life loses all meaning for her. She is irritated by her dull, practical husband, and her children, upon whom she had doted, now seem "like a pair of bothersome beasts that she'd never seen before."

Igawa is cast in the mold of the enigmatic, tormenting, but enthralling man who appears in various guises throughout Takahashi's literature. During their trysts Haruyo would experience the heights of sexual transport, but afterward, when they were out in public, Igawa would treat her cruelly. Baffled and appalled by his contradictory behavior, Haruyo would feel her familiar identity dissolve and another, "demonic" self arise in its place. When a latent side of Haruyo's character, whether lustful or deranged, was aroused by Igawa, her regular seemly façade was shattered. Long after her marriage, Haruyo continues to yearn for the sensation of self-loss that she experienced with Igawa when they were lovers.

The first four stories of the *Lonely Woman* sequence all portray women who are estranged from mainstream life because they have awakened to impulses within them that are at odds with conventional social and gender norms. Although each woman has a rich inner life, her heightened self-awareness also creates agonizing desire — for excitement, knowledge, power, revenge, erotic bliss. In contrast to these women, Yoshimura Ruriko, the protagonist of "Strange Bonds," is a mellow old woman who, although similarly solitary and introspective, has transcended desire and its attendant suffering. Her life has been fraught with hardships and losses, including the deaths of all her family members. As she puts it, "people and things — everything — had been wrenched from her, as if by centrifugal force, and had vanished somewhere." Now her main pastime is simply walking around, reflecting, reminiscing, and observing. But she is not pathetic; she is buoyant. She drifts around like a cloud or a leaf in the wind.

Long ago, when Ruriko was returning by boat to Japan after the war, she had met an eccentric man on board whose gentleness and detachment had touched and intrigued her. She had searched for the man for years, in hopes of learning something from him, but he had eluded her. Toward the end of the story, when her long-cherished dream of meeting the man again suddenly seems within reach, she realizes that it is no longer vital that she do so. Liberated from her last attachment — the desire for a teacher — Ruriko has become her own fountain of wisdom. The story and the entire sequence come to a close with a scene that affirms wisdom and compassion as the fruits of a richly lived earthly life. At the same time, the scene hints at the existence of an eternal realm that has correspondences in this world.

NOTES

1. Takahashi's father, Okamoto Shōjirō, passed away in 1984, and her mother, Okamoto Michiko, in 2000. During a visit with the author in 1997 I expressed surprise that in her many published nonfiction writings to date she never discussed her parents or her relationship with them. She replied that it would be impossible for her to accurately describe individuals whose lives were so intimately enmeshed with hers. Despite her reluctance to broach this topic, she has since written a concise, illuminating essay about her family background entitled "My Genealogy." In it she portrays her parents as utterly different from each other in character: her father pragmatic, mild-mannered, and benign, and her mother artistic, ardent, and unusually volatile. Takahashi feels that her own innate temperament is identical to her mother's, but unlike her, she habitually conceals her intense emotions. Thus in her youth she was often misperceived, by relatives and close friends, as sharing her father's serene disposition.

2. "Kansai" is the term for the district in western Japan that includes Kyoto, Osaka, and the surrounding area.

3. It was not her relationship with Kazumi but the social entanglements and restrictions the marriage entailed, especially when the couple lived in Kyoto, that Takako felt hampered her growth as an individual and a writer. She repeatedly emphasizes in her writings that Kazumi's intellectual companionship, artistic inspiration, emotional support, and encouragement of her literary aspirations were vital to her development, especially in the early years of their marriage. (See, for example, "Takahashi Kazumi and My Literary Career.") Kazumi's decision to accept the job offer at Kyoto University was prompted not so much by the lure of a prestigious post but by the prospect of returning to familiar surroundings. Highly sensitive to criticism, he had been discouraged by some recent negative book reviews. A large, affectionate family in Osaka, where he grew up, and numerous friends

and admirers throughout Kansai were eagerly waiting to welcome him home. For his wife, who was struggling to forge an independent identity, returning to the repressive atmosphere of Kyoto was unthinkable. Stunned by Takako's decision to remain alone in Kamakura, Kazumi responded predictably: he went on a drinking binge and did not return home for several days. But his gentle, tolerant nature no doubt enabled him to quickly resign himself to his wife's decision with little acrimony. Takako, on the other hand, anguished over the consequences of her self-assertive choice. To distract herself from the situation, she took a trip alone, for the first time, to Europe in April 1967, and spent five months traveling around France and various other countries. This brave adventure was fortuitous; it not only lifted her spirits but also had far-reaching effects on her literature and life course. Takahashi Takako discusses the circumstances surrounding her separation from Kazumi in "Social Pressure and So Forth."

4. See "Toward the Ocean of the Unconscious," 564–65. Vivid discussions of various aspects of the cultures of Kyoto and the Kansai district that irritate the author are also found in "Concerning My Neurosis," "Why Does It Turn Into a Drinking Party?" and the above-mentioned "The Kyoto Woman Within Me." Her early short story, "An Old City," is a chilling evocation of the suspiciousness toward outsiders and the evasive style of communication that, in her view, typify Kyotoites.

5. Takahashi gives a detailed account of her years in France, focusing on her experiences in this religious society, in *The Path I Traveled*. She describes, with a mixture of bewilderment, indulgence, and irony, the "human comedy" of the group's gradual descent into chaos and corruption. Despite the exploitation that she herself endured, she has not become embittered, and she is generous in acknowledging the fruits of her involvement with this organization. The author's earlier, purely favorable, perspective on this group is presented in "Commentary on the Jerusalem Order." Further details about the organization, including its official name, "Les Fraternités Monastiques de Jérusalem," are given in "*The Path I Traveled*—Supplement." Here, Takahashi explains the Catholic Church's distinction between "order" and "congregation" and

notes that, strictly speaking, the society in question does not fit the definition of either category. The group had been petitioning to obtain official recognition from the Catholic Church as a "monastic association," but because its efforts had not yet been successful, it had moved its headquarters from Paris to a small, provincial city around the time that Takahashi withdrew from it.

6. "Thoughts on the Concept of the *Doppelgänger*" contains brief commentaries on "William Wilson," *The Picture of Dorian Gray*, *Séraphîta*, and Hoffmann's *The Devil's Elixirs*. Takahashi devotes an entire essay to her reflections on "The Sandman" ("The Mysteriousness of 'The Sandman'") and on *Séraphîta* ("The Mysteriousness of *Séraphîta*"). She has also occasionally written about Japanese literature informed by the theme of the divided self. In "Concerning the Devil," for instance, she describes a play set in ancient Japan that had greatly impressed her. In it, a gentle, innocent woman who has been badly mistreated temporarily turns into a demon and goes on a rampage, murdering and devouring her persecutors (217–19). Takahashi draws a comparison between this tale and her own story in the present collection, "The Suspended Bridge," in which the heroine, who is obsessed with a man who tantalizes her, at times feels that she is possessed by a demon.

7. The unusual title of this novel, whose central character is a Japanese woman musician living in Paris, is taken from J. S. Bach's cantata #115, "Mache dich, mein Geist, bereit" ("Come, my soul, thyself prepare").

Works Cited and Consulted

(Unless otherwise indicated, the place of publication of all works is Tokyo.)

Matsumoto Tōru. "Commentary" ("Kaisetsu"). In *Lonely Woman*, 209–17.

Takahashi Takako. "As I Walk Through the Endless Valley of Woe" ("Tōku, kutsū no tani o aruite iru toki"; 1983). In *Takahashi Takako's Self-Selected Literary Works* (hereafter, *TTSLW*), 4:477–528.

——. "Around the Time of My Baptism" ("Jusen no koro"). *TTSLW* 1:521–42.

——. "Bach in Church" ("Kyōkai no naka no Bahha"; 1975). In *The Darkness of Memory*, 115–19.

——. "Bach's Organ Music" ("Bahha no orugan kyoku"; 1979). In *Startled Flowers*, 62–66.

——. "Captive" ("Toraware"; 1970). In *Yonder Sound of Water*, 57–109.

——. "Ceaseless Encounters" ("Owari naki deai"; 1985). *TTSLW* 3:493–560.

——. *Child of Wrath* (*Ikari no ko*; 1985). *TTSLW* 3:7–230.

——. "Commentary on the Jerusalem Order" ("Erusaremu shūdōkai ni tsuite no kaisetsu"). In *Spiritual Departure*, 181–90.

——. "Concerning the Devil" ("Akuma ni tsuite"; 1978). In *Startled Flowers*, 212–22.

——."Concerning My Neurosis" ("Watashi no noirōze no koto"). In *Remembering Takahashi Kazumi*, 151–59.

——. *The Darkness of Memory* (*Kioku no kurasa*). Kyoto: Jimbun Shoin, 1977.

——. *"The Desert of Love* and God" (*"Ai no sabaku* to kami"; 1979). In *Startled Flowers*, 45–48.

——. "Doll Love" ("Ningyō ai"; 1976). *TTSLW* 4:387–427.

——. *Exile* (*Bōmeisha*). Kōdansha, 1995.

——. "Foxfire" ("Kitsunebi"; 1976). *TTSLW* 1:369–402.

——. "France, My Love" ("Furansu, wa ga ai"; 1996). In *Reflections That Radiate*, 171–74.

——. *The Glorious Day* (*Hanayagu hi*). Kōdansha, 1975.

——. "'Going Mad'" ("'Kuruu'"; 1973). In *Soul Dogs*, 197–206.

——. *The Heavenly Lake* (*Ten no mizuumi*; 1977). *TTSLW* 2:7–206.

——. *The House of Rebirth* (*Yomigaeri no ie*; 1980). *TTSLW* 3:318–450.

——. "The Kyoto Woman Within Me" ("Watashi no naka no kyōonna"; 1975). In *The Darkness of Memory*, 241–45.

——. "A Literature of Murder" ("Satsui no bungaku"; 1973). In *Soul Dogs*, 13–16.

——. "Lonely Woman" ("Ronrii ūman"; 1974). *TTSLW* 1:294–332.

——. *Lonely Woman* (*Ronrii ūman*; 1977). Shūeisha (paperback), 1982.

——. "The Lost Picture" ("Ushinawareta e"; 1973). In *The Lost Picture*, 5–132.

———. *The Lost Picture* (*Ushinawareta e*). Kawade Shobō Shinsha, 1974.

———. *Memories of Takahashi Kazumi* (*Takahashi Kazumi no omoide*). Kōsōsha, 1977.

———. "My Genealogy" ("Watashi no kakei"). In *These Twilight Years*, 15–25.

———. "The Mysteriousness of 'The Sandman'" ("'Suna otoko' no shimpi"; 1974). In *Soul Dogs*, 44–48.

———. "The Mysteriousness of *Séraphîta*" ("*Serafīta* no shimpi"; 1978). In *Startled Flowers*, 17–21.

———. "An Old City" ("Mukashi no machi"; 1974). In *The Glorious Day*, 85–134.

———. "The Oracle" ("Otsuge"; 1975). *TTSLW* 1:333–68.

———. "Passing Through the 'Dark Night'" ("An'ya o tōtte"). *TTSLW* 4:529–52.

———. *The Path I Traveled* (*Watashi no tōtta michi*). Kōdansha, 1999.

———. "*The Path I Traveled*—Supplement" ("*Watashi no tōtta michi*—hoi"). In *These Twilight Years*, 134–36.

———. *Prepare Thyself, My Soul* (*Yosooi seyo, waga tamashii yo*; 1982). *TTSLW* 4:7–382.

———. "Reflections on My Maiden Work" ("Shojosaku e no kaiki"; 1974). In *Soul Dogs*, 165–67.

———. *Reflections That Radiate* (*Hōsha suru omoi*). Kōdansha, 1997.

———. *Remembering Takahashi Kazumi: Twenty-Five Years Later* (*Takahashi Kazumi to iu hito: nijūgo-nen no ato ni*). Kawade Shobō Shinsha, 1997.

———. *A Ruined Landscape* (*Botsuraku fūkei*). Kawade Shobō Shinsha, 1974.

———. "Self-Compiled Chronological Record" [of the author's life and career] ("Jihitsu nenpu"). *TTSLW* 4:553–79.

———. "Sexuality: The Demonic and the Maternal in Women" ("Sei—onna ni okeru mashō to bosei"; 1976). In *The Darkness of Memory*, 86–99.

———. "Social Pressure and So Forth" ("Shakaiteki atsuryoku unnun no koto"). In *Remembering Takahashi Kazumi*, 160–64.

———. *Soul Dogs* (*Tamashii no inu*). Kōdansha, 1975.

———. *Spiritual Departure* (*Reiteki na shuppatsu*). Joshi Pauro Kai, 1985.

——. *Startled Flowers* (*Odoroita hana*). Kyoto: Jimbun Shoin, 1980.

——. "Strange Bonds" ("Fushigi na en"; 1977). *TTSLW* 1:441–74.

——. "Supplement" ("Furoku"). In *Child of Wrath* (*Ikari no ko*). Kōdansha, 1985.

——. "The Suspended Bridge" ("Tsuribashi"; 1977). *TTSLW* 1:403–40.

——. "Symbiotic Space" ("Kyōsei kūkan"; 1971). In *Symbiotic Space*, 5–50.

——. *Symbiotic Space* (*Kyōsei kūkan*). Shinchōsha, 1973.

——. "Takahashi Kazumi and My Literary Career" ("Takahashi Kazumi to sakka to shite no watashi"). In *Memories of Takahashi Kazumi*, 91–98.

——. *Takahashi Takako's Self-Selected Literary Works* (*Takahashi Takako jisen shōsetsushū*). 4 vols. Kōdansha, 1994.

——. *The Tempter* (*Yūwakusha*; 1976). *TTSLW* 1:7–291.

——. "This World as a 'Wasteland'" ("Kono yo no 'arano'"). *TTSLW* 2:535–58.

——. *These Twilight Years* (*Kono bannen to iu toki*). Kōdansha, 2002.

——. "Thoughts on the Concept of the *Doppelgänger*" ("Dopperugengeru-kō"; 1974). In *Soul Dogs*, 39–43.

——. *To the End of the Sky* (*Sora no hate made*). Shinchōsha, 1973.

——. "To Love" ("Kou"; 1984). *TTSLW* 3:451–92.

——. "Toward the Ocean of the Unconscious" ("Senzai suru umi e"). *TTSLW* 3:561–83.

——. *Wasteland* (*Arano*; 1980). *TTSLW* 2:255–533.

——. "Why Does It Turn Into a Drinking Party?" ("Naze shuen ni naru no ka"). In *Remembering Takahashi Kazumi*, 78–85.

——. "Why I Became a Catholic" ("Naze katorikku ni natta ka"; 1977). In *Startled Flowers*, 183–88.

——. "Yonder Sound of Water" ("Kanata no mizu oto"; 1971). In *Yonder Sound of Water*, 203–74.

——. *Yonder Sound of Water* (*Kanata no mizu oto*). Kōdansha, 1971.

Note on This Translation

My aim has been to produce a literary translation of *Lonely Woman* while preserving, when possible and desirable, the literal meaning of the original text. I have striven for fidelity to the content, spirit, tone, and impact of the original, even when this entailed deviating somewhat from its words or form. Japanese and English are utterly different languages in many respects. To begin with, their syntax is completely different. Moreover, extremely long sentences are common in Japanese, and Japanese linguistic expression tends to be rather imprecise and ambiguous in contrast to English. In my translation I have employed natural English syntax. I have often divided long Japanese sentences into two English sentences and have routinely used more exact expressions to clarify what is merely suggested in the original, when it seemed that to do so would better convey the effects of the passage in question than using a correspondingly vague expression. I have sometimes modified metaphors rather than translating them literally. Takahashi Takako uses many single-sentence paragraphs, especially in extended passages of dialogue. While I have generally maintained the paragraph divisions of the original text, I have combined two or more single-sentence paragraphs into one when it seemed more natural in English to do so.

The unstable narrative viewpoint in *Lonely Woman* posed a challenge to render in a coherent, relatively unobtrusive way. It is quite common in Japanese literary works that are predominantly third-person, past-tense narratives for the narrator and the protagonist to alternately converge and separate. Suddenly the narrator disappears and the reader is plunged into the protagonist's stream of consciousness. Then the narrator reemerges and resumes her role as intermediary between protagonist and reader. In English, the intermingling of first- and third-person narrative perspectives and of past and present verb tenses can be jarring. I have tried to smooth out these inconsistencies by occasionally altering verb tenses, inserting "she thought," and so forth. But I have not attempted to completely unify the narrative perspective, because these "border crossings" are pervasive and also, I think, thematically meaningful.

Takahashi regularly uses XXs or oos in addresses and phone numbers so as to avoid compromising the privacy of any individual or organization that might, coincidentally, have the same address or phone number. I have maintained her custom in the translation. I have also retained the conventional order of Japanese names, surname preceding given name.

Lonely Woman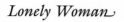

Lonely Woman

In the midst of her dream, Sakiko was dimly conscious of letting out a long moan. The moan was emerging, like something being squeezed out, from some obscure place deep inside her body. Just before reaching her mouth it stopped short, and to her irritation, it wouldn't come out. The moan welled up again and again at regular intervals. Although it didn't escape her lips, it produced an audible sound. That sound grew louder and louder until the mounting pressure in her chest finally woke Sakiko up.

Fire engines seemed to be approaching, their sirens wailing over and over.

As she listened to that sound, which she couldn't yet distinguish from her moan, Sakiko turned face up in bed and peered through the darkness. The terrain around here was sinuous. Often it would sound as if a fire engine was approaching, but suddenly the wail of its siren would swerve off and subside. The area was tightly hemmed in by rings of small mountains, so a siren emitted by a distant vehicle would reverberate among the mountains and sometimes sound deceptively close by.

The first fire engine's siren ceased. Sakiko, whose entire attention had been focused on that sound, guessed that the vehicle had stopped on the other side of the mountain. This house, where she was renting a second-story room, stood on a bluff, and the road in front of it circled halfway around the mountain. She imagined the fire engine on the other side, partly because of a strange building over there that sometimes caught her attention when she passed it while out on a walk. The building, which resembled a slightly outdated company dormitory, was deserted and looked rather incongruous. Its tin roof was so green that one might mistake the color for verdigris. For some reason, it was that building which Sakiko now pictured as being wreathed in flames.

Suddenly she heard loud popping noises, like the sound of bamboo canes bursting open. She instantly leaped out of bed, thinking it was a mountain fire. Rain hadn't fallen for fifty-one days straight, and the winter mountains were completely dried out.

When she opened the wooden shutters, her entire field of vision was engulfed in bright crimson flames that were shooting up and evaporating with a thunderous roar. It wasn't a mountain fire. The house next door was on fire. Those mysterious popping noises continued without abating. At first she'd thought it was the sound of the parched trees on the mountains splitting apart as they burned. But when she stuck her head out of the second-floor window and looked down on the road, she realized that the noises were coming from a hose being unreeled from a fire engine that was parked there. "What should I do?" she murmured. The landlord and landlady were away for two weeks. If the fire spread here from the neighbor's home, Sakiko would be partly responsible. But the words "What should I do?" had merely sprung to her lips automatically at the sight of the fire, and Sakiko didn't budge from the spot. The things in this rented room were her only worldly possessions, but she felt no impulse to try to protect them. She just stood by the window, entranced by the sight of the encroaching flames.

Since there was no breeze, the pillar of fire rose straight toward the sky. Just as it was turning into a sheet of flame, it suddenly shattered into countless fine sparks that continued to shoot upward. The entire spectacle seemed to be making a roaring sound, yet at the same time to be a silent drama of color and shapes. Sakiko gazed at the dire scene before her eyes with a sense of urgency, but that sense was at odds with her feeling of being rooted to the spot. The brilliant hue of the pillar of fire gradually suffused the entire sky, creating a crimson panorama. Against that backdrop the silhouette of the house next door slowly emerged. *Why, no! It's not the house next door that's on fire!* When this dawned on Sakiko, she again thrust her head out the window.

A steady stream of people was filing down the street through the darkness, which had turned into a reddish-black haze. Why, at this hour of night? They weren't walking in groups, but one by one. Perhaps that was why each person looked strangely forlorn, strangely expressionless, as he emerged from the pitch-darkness into the light cast by the fire, was illuminated for a moment, then vanished, as if plunging into the darkness. Even after she realized that these people were on their way to gape at the fire, Sakiko couldn't shake off the eerie feeling aroused in her by the sight of people walking singly, one after another. Perhaps each person who'd rushed out of his home to gawk at the fire had dashed out alone without thinking, and was now bewildered to find himself walking alone in the middle of the night.

If the fire wasn't next door, then where was it? On the other side of Sakiko's neighbor's house was an elementary school. But why should there be a fire late at night at a deserted elementary school? After assuring herself that there was no wind and also that plenty of fire engines had assembled, Sakiko snuggled down in her bed again, immediately forgot about the fire and everything else, and fell into a sound sleep. Then, at the threshold of her consciousness, again she could hear sirens wailing and merging with her moan. Finally, the whole blend of sensations swerved up diagonally through her dream and subsided.

"MY GOODNESS, it was dreadful, wasn't it? I was a nervous wreck wondering what would happen. I was the first one to notice it. Did you realize that it was I who was going around knocking on the gates of your house and the ones across the street, crying 'Fire! Fire!'?"

The moment she saw Sakiko, the old woman who lived alone next door barraged her. She was obviously worked up; her ordinarily shrill voice sounded all the shriller to Sakiko.

"What's this crowd doing here?" Sakiko asked, stopping just outside her gate. Unlike the people she'd seen last night, drifting through the darkness like ghosts, today there were people casually standing around from here all the way up the road, as far as she could see. At this hour, just past seven o'clock, when Sakiko always passed through her gate on her way to work, she was used to seeing only office workers striding along through the crisp morning air, with resolute looks on their faces.

"Can you imagine how I felt? There was a fire roaring right in front of my house! Oh, of course, my yard is big. And there wasn't a breeze, either. But the problem is the mountains. If the fire were to spread to the mountains, my house, naturally, and yours too, and everything around here would be burned to ashes, don't you see?" The old woman's voice rose melodramatically on the final syllable.

"Why are all these people standing around here?" Sakiko asked again. The old woman had ignored her question and just kept venting her own feelings. If it were only the people in their neighborhood, it would be understandable. But many people whom Sakiko had never seen before were clustered together and talking, as if conferring with each other.

"Oh yes, indeed they are. The elementary school gymnasium burned to the ground. The parents must be worried to death," said the old woman, putting her own slant on the matter. Then she shrieked, "Oh, Missus!" and made a beeline for the housewife standing diagonally across from them. Two other housewives whom Sakiko recognized were standing with that woman.

"In fifty-one days it hasn't rained a drop, you know. It was like throwing a lit match into a pile of firewood. In no time at all it burned to the ground."

"My dear, today is the fifty-*second* day," crowed the old woman's voice.

"What in the world is going on? Nothing but fine weather day after day."

"Apparently it's going to continue for some time. I hear there's no sign of rain for the rest of the month."

"They say just throwing a lit cigarette into the mountains would make them go up in flames. Well, thank heavens that sparks didn't fly last night."

"Dear, do you remember the mountain fire we had five years ago?" The old woman's eyes widened behind her silver-rimmed glasses.

"That must have been before we moved here."

"Goodness, it was dreadful. Look—that mountain over there— do you see? There's not a single tree in sight, is there. Because at that time they were all destroyed. Do you know that lone farm-house on the edge of the river? Well, they tore down the barn over there and set it on fire. A sheet of newspaper that was on fire float- ed off, and even though it's awfully far away, the scrap was caught up by the wind and sailed straight off and landed on top of that mountain. It was evening. That night the mountain turned bright red and kept right on burning. I don't know how many fire engines came. Sirens were blaring from all directions. What with the fire and the sirens, I was dashing in and out, in and out. Naturally, I didn't sleep a wink all night. After all, I'm a woman living alone, you know. Not that there was any danger that the fire would spread all the way to my house. But I'm a woman living alone, after all. Oh, that's right. That time too—I remember now—I went from house to house spreading the word. I cried, 'Fire! Fire!'"

The old woman mimed, with exaggerated gestures, how she had knocked on each and every gate. Her shrill voice contrasted oddly with the elegant effect created by her lovely white hair and impeccable kimono.

"How did yesterday's fire start?"

"It was because it hasn't rained for fifty-two days. When the air gets so dry that even your throat is parched, it's no wonder if suddenly something just bursts into flame."

"What a strange thing to say!"

"If it doesn't rain for the rest of the month, there'll be tongues of fire spurting from everyone's mouth, mark my words. Anyway, I'm parched right down to my innards."

"If it doesn't rain for another ten days, it will be the first time in the history of the weather station, they say."

"My intuition tells me that there's no chance of the drought ending in ten days. This fine weather will last another twenty or thirty days. You wait and see. Bad luck brings more bad luck. Rain, indeed!"

Intrigued by the old woman's words, Sakiko stood listening for a while, then quickly walked off.

As she passed along her next-door neighbor's hedge, heading toward the elementary school, she saw groups of people who looked like parents standing in clusters. The buzzing of their voices filled the road. No rain in fifty-two days . . . fine weather continuing without even a cloudy day . . . dried-out houses and mountains. . . . Those same phrases, repeated over and over, kept grazing Sakiko's ears.

The school gymnasium, reduced to blackened pillars, ridges, and beams, stood desolately near the roadside on the school grounds. White vapor was rising into the cold air from the charred, water-drenched pieces of wood. Firemen were still tramping around the muddy school grounds in galoshes. Sakiko walked toward the gymnasium, mesmerized by the sight of the building that had undergone such a transformation in a single night. She'd grown used to seeing it nearly every day, on her way to and from work and when she was out for a walk. It was astonishing that in a mere hour it had been utterly demolished like this. If someone had happened to be present, he would surely have become a lump of charcoal no different from the charcoal into which the building had turned. The morning sky, visible through the black ruins, augured clear, brilliant blue skies for later that day.

The mountains behind the elementary school seemed to move along with Sakiko as she walked. The branches of the elm, oak, and cherry trees, now bare of leaves, looked as dry as if they were stage scenery. The bases of the tall grasses were so dry that they seemed to be coated with white powder. If there'd been a wind last night, what would have happened? Sakiko could almost hear the old woman next door crying, "Mountain fire! Mountain fire!" her shrill voice echoing through the cruel blue sky.

SLOWLY, DRAGGING HER BODY like a piece of heavy luggage, Sakiko trudged home that night along the dark road. Since graduating from university she'd been working at a company for six years. Her interest in her job had gradually ebbed, like an evening tide, until she felt as if she'd suddenly found herself standing alone on a deserted beach at dusk. The phrase "I'm so bored" sometimes slipped from her mouth in a voice that was as listless as a yawn. Suddenly she recalled the long moan that had welled up again and again from deep within her body during her dream the night before. The moan hadn't sounded as if it could be coming from her, but rather as if some dark beast were emitting it. But when she awoke, in the daylight there was no beast in sight. There was only herself, a person who became bored with whatever she did.

She was walking home along the dark road with the collar of her coat turned up. As she crossed a stone bridge, she caught the scent of stagnant water rising from the darkness beneath her. The riverbed was deeply hollowed out, and the slope leading to it was steep. Ordinarily she could hear the sound of rushing water here. But since it hadn't rained, there was just a hint of moisture in the odor coming from the rotten leaves lying on the riverbed. Sakiko walked slowly along the winding road that ran past the school grounds. It was almost nine o'clock, so the road was nearly deserted. There was just the sound of her high heels, clicking in a steady rhythm on the pavement. The only structure in sight was the charred skeleton of the gymnasium, which emanated a strange, unearthly air. There was a breeze tonight. A peculiar tension seemed to linger in the ruins at the desolate site of the fire. Was it because Sakiko was imagining the vivid spectacle of the fire superimposed on the scene before her eyes? A foul odor, produced by the various objects that had burned together, was also still faintly wafting around.

After she'd walked a bit farther, she looked back and viewed the scene from the opposite angle. The charred framework resembled a skull with its mouth agape. She walked along the long hedge in front of her next-door neighbor's house. Up ahead, where the hedge ended, the cinder block fence of the home where she rented a room seemed to be floating, as it glowed faintly in the darkness.

Sakiko sensed someone behind her and turned around. The silhouette of a man was approaching. His footsteps sounded as if he were following her. That was probably because he was wearing canvas shoes. Even so, she couldn't help but feel that the man was walking directly toward her. He wore a jacket, and perhaps because he was warmly dressed, his upper body looked terribly puffed up. The man came straight at her, both hands shoved into his pockets.

"I'm from the police." The man spoke in a low voice, as if to ensure the privacy of their conversation. His breath turned white in the cold air.

"Miss Namioka?" In complete contrast to his tone of voice, which suggested concern for her privacy, he stood so close to her that their noses were practically touching.

"No, I'm renting a room in the Namiokas' house." Sakiko looked the man over as she spoke. Nothing identified him as a police officer.

"May I come in? It's cold for you out here, isn't it? It's windy tonight." The man said this after glancing at Sakiko, who was clenching her collar with both hands and standing with her legs pressed together.

"Who are you?"

"I'm a police investigator."

"But what do you want?"

"That's what I'm about to tell you. Earlier today I went around to every house in your neighborhood, but you weren't home, so I've come back at this hour."

"You were waiting for me?"

"Not only that; I've been observing you." As if to emphasize his point, the man looked back at the road that ran toward the elementary school. The night sky was a cold, cloudless expanse. The only difference between day and night was that one sky was blue and the other starry. Day and night, not a cloud nor any haze marred the sky; the fair weather went on endlessly. When this occurred to Sakiko, the sky started looking eerily like a faceless monster.

"Is something wrong?" Sakiko asked, as she went alone through the iron gate.

"There's been an arson." The man's tone of voice became sterner.

"Then I have nothing to tell you," said Sakiko, and she inserted her key into the lock of the gate.

"Did you notice anyone suspicious? Last night, I mean?" The man placed his hand on the gate.

"Are you really from the police?" Sakiko was shivering from the cold as she stood facing the man over the low iron gate.

"There've been two other fires that were started by the same method. All of them were at elementary schools. In every case, oil was used." The man's round face and stocky body were fully illuminated by the lamp at the garden gate.

"Who set them?" asked Sakiko, feeling herself becoming strangely excited.

"If I knew that, I wouldn't be standing here at this time of night."

"No, I mean, was it a man or a woman?" Sakiko asked. She had a flash of self-revelation.

"That's a strange thing to say. If I don't know who did it, how could I know whether it was a man or a woman?"

"I think it was a woman."

"Oh, do you now! And why is that?"

"It's just a hunch."

"But you speak with such conviction. So you did see someone suspicious last night." The man removed a cigarette from his breast pocket and lit it. In the freezing night air the red tip of the cigarette looked hard and sharp.

"I'm cold. I catch colds easily. I'll have to excuse myself now." Sakiko took five or six steps over the flagstone path and stopped at the front door of the house.

"Wait right there," the man said, his tone unexpectedly firm.

"Do you have more to ask? If it's about the arson incident, I don't know a thing." Sakiko was fishing her keys out of her handbag as she spoke.

"I'd like to ask a few more questions. Can I step inside?"

"Please come back tomorrow. It's Saturday, so I'm off work."

"No, this can't wait. There might be a fire again tonight." The man spoke quickly. He pulled the front zipper of his jacket down halfway, and from his inside pocket he pulled out something like a notepad.

"Why would there be a fire tonight?" asked Sakiko, her interest aroused. As she spoke, her fingertips examined the ring of keys that she'd removed for the shape of the key to the front door.

"If the arsonist is the same guy as before, he always sets two fires at the same school."

"You keep saying that. Believe me, it's a woman." Sakiko unlocked the door with her key and began to go inside.

"If you have any idea, please don't hesitate to speak up. I can assure you that it won't cause any trouble for you." The man leaned forward over the gate.

"It's past nine o'clock. Besides, I don't even know if you're a police officer or not," said Sakiko as she began closing the door.

"Look at this. It's a police identification badge," the man appealed.

Sakiko caught a split-second glimpse of the man's white breath and the pad that he was holding out, just before the door closed.

ON HER DAYS OFF, Sakiko slept late. The landlord and landlady were out of town, so she was alone in the large house, and it was silent all morning. That silence blended with the cold and numbed her to the bone. The house stood right beside a mountain, so its chilliness was more penetrating than that of most homes.

She'd felt almost no interest in the fire, except as a spectacle of crimson flames raging in the darkness. But because of her conversation last night with that man who was apparently a police investigator, she had the strange feeling that the fire had insinuated its way into her consciousness. She washed her face, then immediately went out and stood in front of the gate. Instinctively, she began heading toward the elementary school. As she walked along the hedge in front of her next-door neighbor's home, she noted that today, unlike the previous morning, there was no crowd. Only the white, slightly winding pavement stretched on ahead of her. The house next door was much larger than the one where she was renting a room. The purely Japanese-style edifice where the old woman lived alone stood there with a dignified air. Sakiko conjured up a hazy image of the woman. She was always carefully dressed in traditional attire. But whenever Sakiko heard that shrill, nervous voice emitting its steady stream of babble, she sensed turbulent emotions, which the old woman could scarcely contain, seething beneath her refined exterior. Sometimes at night, from her second-floor room, Sakiko would gaze next door, where lights were still on. The lights were on, but she never heard human voices. Because the old woman lived alone. And yet Sakiko always imagined the old woman sitting in the middle of her large house late at night, chattering gaily in her shrill voice, and the house teeming with that inaudible chatter.

After passing the house next door, Sakiko heard clamor coming from the direction of the elementary school up ahead. Ordinarily she would leave her home early in the morning and return in the evening, so she hardly ever heard anything. But on Saturday morning, when she was home from work, sometimes noise drifted all the way to her room. Sakiko disliked the din that came from the elementary school, the high-pitched shrieks of the young children scattering in all directions.

The charred gymnasium came into view. Against the background of the blue sky it looked all the blacker, and its insides were gutted. It still had a sinister air about it, probably because Sakiko imagined it wreathed in fierce flames. The racket was coming from the classroom building. The din, which sounded full of irritation and also made the hearer feel irritated, drifted from the entire building. Just then, the spectacle of children trapped in the burning gymnasium, emitting piercing screams, flashed across Sakiko's mind.

Sakiko averted her eyes from that scene and turned right down a road. She came to a house with a long white wooden fence. The old woman who lived next door to her was standing at the back door to that house.

"Because I have sharp ears. Anyway, I'm a woman living alone, after all. In the middle of the night, just the click of a single dry leaf dropping to the ground is enough to wake me up. When I heard that crackling sound of fire, I sat bolt upright. But no one else had realized it yet. Even though there was a pillar of fire blazing up, nobody had come out of his house. I was the first one to rush out, you know, and I went around from door to door knocking and crying, 'Fire! Fire!'"

The old woman was talking to the housewife at the house with the white wooden fence. She was probably saying the same thing to everyone she met.

"Well hello, Miss Namioka! Out for a stroll?" When the old woman noticed Sakiko, her face lit up in a friendly smile. She always addressed Sakiko by her landlord's surname. Sakiko simply bowed politely. If she let herself be detained, she would be subjected to endless chatter.

"Fine weather again today—isn't it disgusting? This makes the fifty-third day. Mark my word, it's going to last for sixty, even seventy days. It's ridiculous to have so much fine weather."

The old woman faced Sakiko and bowed formally over and over.

Sakiko passed, then after she'd gone a bit farther, the friendly voice pursued her. "You haven't heard yet, have you? It was arson! They say the culprit is watching for another chance. Next time it will be the classroom building. And if that happens, there's sure to be a mountain fire."

Sakiko turned in the direction of the lively voice, bowed again, then kept walking.

She had come out to look at the aftermath of the fire without even eating breakfast. She felt as though the old woman's chatter had dissipated her strange obsession with the fire, so she circled around the neighborhood, then headed back to her home.

"I'm sorry to have bothered you last night." A man was standing in front of Sakiko's gate. He looked the same as last night, but indeed, he did seem to be a police officer.

"I just went to have a look at the site of the fire," said Sakiko, laughing slightly.

"You seem to be awfully interested in it." The investigator kept a perfectly straight face and stared sharply at her.

"Interested?" she rejoined. She pictured the young children burning, packed together in the blazing gymnasium.

"I came again because I sensed that you had some information that could be useful to us." The officer winked.

"Well, step inside, then. But as far as useful information goes, I have nothing to offer." Sakiko invited him in because she was eager to know about the arsonist.

The man sat on the step in the front hall and began smoking a cigarette. He took a puff or two, and then, with the cigarette poised in midair, he fell silent. The back of his bulky jacket bulged up right before Sakiko's eyes. As she faced that back, which seemed to be bottling up thoughts that its owner wanted to express, Sakiko struggled to suppress her curiosity. She felt as if it was about to erupt from her throat like the twittering of a pigeon.

"Well?" said Sakiko, taking the initiative.

"To come to the point, did you see something?" The man ignored her question and directed his own question at her.

"Is that what they call a 'police pad'?" Sakiko looked at the badge holder that the policeman was toying with in the hand that wasn't holding the cigarette.

"I believe you said it was a woman, didn't you?" The investigator, who had been keeping his back to Sakiko, finally turned to look at her. His piercing gaze bore straight into her.

"I did say that. So how in the world did the woman execute the crime?" asked Sakiko, her own direct gaze challenging the officer's.

"We don't know whether or not it's a woman."

"Didn't you say the person is focusing on elementary schools?"

"Yes; this is the third incident."

"Why?"

"You'd have to ask the arsonist that one."

"I know perfectly well."

"You do?"

"Of course."

The investigator stifled a response, turned his back to Sakiko again, and leaned forward. The cigarette between his fingertips continued to burn, and the elongated ash, heavy as feathery snowflakes, dropped to the ground. The man finally noticed, and he tapped the cigarette with his fingertip to make more ash fall off.

Sakiko began laughing.

"What is it?" The investigator looked at her.

"It's a concrete floor, so you don't have to worry. Since it hasn't rained in fifty-three days, all it would take is that cigarette to make this house go up in flames." Sakiko struggled to contain her mirth.

"This isn't the first year that an elementary school has been the target of arson. It's happened every year for a long time. Schools in general are likely targets, even junior high and high schools," said the man, ignoring Sakiko's snickers.

"Only at night?"

"It's happened during the day, too."

"Are there fires at elementary schools during the daytime?" Sakiko asked. Again she envisioned countless young children shrieking, roasting to a crisp in that inferno with no exit.

"I said that this is the third incident in the case, didn't I? Assuming that the arsonist is the same person. He sets two fires each time. Did I tell you this?"

"Did the schools burn to the ground?"

"In the initial instance, yes. First he set fire to the gymnasium, then the classroom building. Those two fires destroyed everything."

"Was the second incident the same?"

"No, those fires were set during the day, and they only amounted to small ones."

"During the day? That's strange, isn't it?"

"What is?"

"It's risky, isn't it? For the criminal. An elementary school is a place with lots of people. The criminal would be caught, wouldn't she?"

"That's what puzzles me, too. The method was the same—oil was used—but even though it was daytime, no one saw anyone suspicious."

"Oh, now I get it. It's simple." Sakiko became animated.

"Again, you speak with conviction."

Maybe because he was staring hard at her, the man seemed to be squinting.

"But the arsons at night. . . . What in the world drives a person to set fire to a deserted elementary school?"

During this conversation, Sakiko had suddenly grown so excited that her chest ached. She now regretted not having gone to the scene of the fire the night before last. She hadn't witnessed the actual sight of the gymnasium in flames, because the house next door had blocked her view of the building.

"What drives a person? That varies, according to the statistics. These days prices are high, and we're in a recession. People feel frustrated or they suddenly get the urge to vent their feelings. . . . That's usually how it happens." The officer kept a businesslike, expressionless face as he delivered his explanation.

"Setting fire at night to an elementary school would be a perfect solution. Anyway, the blaze would be enormous. Enormous and magnificent." Sakiko spoke as if she were viewing the spectacle through the eyes of the arsonist.

"Even an arsonist has an ethical sense. If he sets fire to an elementary school at night, only the buildings will burn."

"But the second incident was during the day, wasn't it? She set the buildings on fire at a time when they were filled with pupils. Was it the same arsonist as the first time?" Sakiko asked, leaning forward slightly.

"I said before, didn't I? The method was the same."

The man lit yet another cigarette. Many stamped-out cigarette butts lay on the concrete floor.

"You said the person used oil, didn't you," said Sakiko. She felt as if she could smell that pungent odor, which was neither quite pleasant nor unpleasant.

"Apparently the guy filled an empty pocket flask of whiskey with oil and took it with him. Each time an empty bottle was found at the scene of the fire. When the fire ignited, he slipped away quickly. Like the wind. Anyway, no one noticed him."

"Slipped away quickly? Why?"

"It's obvious, isn't it?"

"That's not what the woman did."

"'The woman'—you're still convinced that it was a woman, aren't you?"

"At the end of the school day, while the little pupils were still making a commotion, the woman poured the oil and lit the fire, then she slowly walked down the corridor. All around her, pupils were scampering past and teachers were walking by. Everyone had a chance to get a good look at her. But she sauntered along, coolly and slowly, and went out. That's the sort of criminal she is." Sakiko found herself becoming more eloquent than usual.

"Well now, that's remarkable reasoning." Despite his remark, the investigator didn't turn to look at Sakiko. He just kept staring at a single point on the front door.

"Remarkable?"

"No, it's my job, so I'm well aware of that much. But I'm saying that for you, it's remarkable."

"I'm glad if I've been of any help."

Sakiko felt a bit drained. Perhaps it was because she'd gotten so caught up in being the arsonist. She began to feel chilled. The entryway was unheated.

"Will this do? The landlord is away, so I shouldn't let anyone stay here too long," she said, standing up.

"Do you use an oil heater here?" The officer rose too, and spoke without turning around.

"Why?" Sakiko was a bit startled by the question.

"I'm just asking everyone." The man gripped the doorknob.

"Did someone in this neighborhood set the fires?"

As Sakiko pronounced the words "someone in this neighborhood," she suddenly felt agitated. She was one of the people in the neighborhood. She listened intently, as if trying to catch the sound of that agitation. She seemed to hear, welling up from some dark hollow deep within her, that moaning she'd heard in her dream. She stood in a daze, savoring the vague sensation that it was the arsonist who was moaning.

"Is there a bicycle here?" The investigator spoke again, as he finally turned the knob and opened the door.

"I think the landlord has an old bicycle in the shed."

After the man had left, Sakiko stared steadily at the cigarette butts lying on the concrete floor of the entryway. She counted them mechanically—one, two, three. In contrast, her head reeled feverishly as the imaginary arsonist began stirring within her. Sakiko was starting to feel unbalanced, as if she had lost her moorings.

AROUND TEN O'CLOCK AT NIGHT Sakiko suddenly decided to go out. She had a hunch that the arsonist was roaming around in the pitch-darkness. Riding a beat-up bicycle, coming out of nowhere, cutting diagonally through the empty night, she was approaching lightly. The pungent odor of oil rose from the inner pocket of her coat. She was circling around and around the neighborhood, mildly intoxicated by that odor, and passionately intoxicated by the crime she was about to commit. If the same person walked past the same place over and over she would arouse suspicion, but if she were riding a bicycle, she wouldn't. Who knows, it might even be someone living in the neighborhood. If she were riding a bicycle, she could also pretend to be someone who'd come from a distance. A woman like her would wear a wool cap, pulled down close to her eyes, and she'd circle around and around, gradually zeroing in on her objective. The investigator had spoken of high prices and economic recession. He'd also mentioned being frustrated and acting on impulse. No, those weren't the reasons, thought Sakiko. Why, then?

She stood up in her room, in order to go out. Just then, inside her, Sakiko felt that kind of woman stand up. Anyway, she would go to the scene of the fire. The arsonist had set fires twice at the same location, so maybe tonight Sakiko would be able to meet her. When she went out into the hall, a cold blast of air struck her cheek. If you stood still outdoors at ten o'clock at night in February, you'd probably be chilled through, she thought.

It occurred to her to cover her head with a large shawl that was meant to be worn with a kimono. She opened her closet and took out one box of clothing after another. When she reached the box on the bottom she dragged it out. She hadn't worn traditional clothing for the past two or three years, so it was stored away.

When she opened the box, she caught a whiff of mothballs. During the time that she wasn't using the garments, she hadn't changed the mothballs, so the clothes gave off a stale, dusty odor. She pulled out the large, imitation-fur shawl. The old newspaper covering it was brittle. On the bottom of the box was another newspaper, neatly folded in a rectangle that exactly matched the shape of the box. She glanced at it.

The headline LONELY WOMAN caught her attention. She noticed that the date on the newspaper was 1966. Evidently it had been placed in the box much earlier than the newspaper that had covered the shawl. Sakiko felt strangely attracted to that headline. As she leaned over the box, she began reading the article. It was in the Home section of the paper.

In the foggy city of London, you sometimes see a certain type of woman. She is no longer young, nor is she old; it's hard to judge her age. Usually she is walking by herself. She leans slightly forward as she trots along, clicking her heels, through that turbid city where the sun never shines because of the fog. She wanders around through the huge metropolis as if she has nothing to do. I could always spot such women, no matter where they were. Because they all bore the same mark. They exuded a peculiar blend of decay and vigor. It wasn't that they shared a certain occupation. It wasn't that they shared a certain social status. It wasn't that they shared a certain physical resemblance. Even when they were laughing, that mark remained visible through their laughter. Even when they were eating, that brand stood out on their hunched backs like a birthmark. I noticed such women in every social class. It wasn't that they constituted a separate class. There is only one phrase to describe such a woman. In the sprawling city of London she is called a "lonely woman."

Sakiko raised her head from the clothes box and murmured in a low voice, "lonely woman."

She stood up, but her desire to wrap the large shawl around her head and go out to meet the arsonist had vanished. Standing stiffly in the middle of the room, she uttered that phrase again. The words were engraved in her mind. Her voice bore no trace of the dampness mentioned in the article; rather, she pronounced the words dryly. "Lonely woman." That was the name of the imaginary female arsonist.

WHEN SAKIKO OPENED THE RAIN SHUTTERS, the dazzling afternoon sunlight seemed to pierce her eyes. It was Sunday, so the air didn't reverberate with the shouts of the elementary school children. The old woman next door was out on her veranda. When Sakiko opened her rain shutters, the sound made her look up in Sakiko's direction. As usual, from early morning she was already meticulously dressed in a kimono, and despite the cold, she stood perfectly erect. She was holding a birdcage in her right hand.

"Well, if this isn't something. This makes one more day. Fifty-four days. Splendid weather, indeed! It's imperial weather, as they say. Miss Namioka, do you know that expression—'imperial weather'? It means a clear blue sky without a single cloud, just like today's. Day after day, we're blessed with imperial weather, lucky us! Imagine how dry the mountains must be getting! Can't you almost hear the sound of flames crackling! Just look at that!"

The old woman faced the mountain that lay just beyond her yard, raised her hand that wasn't holding the birdcage, and gestured toward it. Her shrill voice rang out gaily, as if she could hardly wait for the mountains to burst into flames. The second floor where Sakiko was standing and the first-floor veranda where the old woman was were quite far apart, but that voice carried well. It was a voice that resounded through the entire neighborhood, day in and day out. The old woman who lived alone would buttonhole anyone and bombard them with chatter. Layer upon layer of dried-out wild bamboo was growing on the cliff to which the woman had just pointed. It leaned toward her yard.

"Miss Namioka, what do you think of this?" asked the old woman, changing the subject. She lifted up the cage. Inside was a black bird that looked like a baby crow.

Sakiko remained silent. Her voice never had much volume, so if she tried to carry on a conversation with the woman at this distance, she'd probably exhaust herself.

"This is a mynah bird. It's a bird that mimics people's voices. Someone brought it to me this morning." The old woman prattled on to herself.

"It must be quite a job to care for so many of them," Sakiko managed to say.

"What's that?" Apparently the woman couldn't hear Sakiko's fragile voice. She cupped her hand over her ear in an exaggerated gesture, as if straining to hear.

"You're going to keep another one, even though you already have so many?" Sakiko was forced to exert her feeble voice.

"There aren't any others. They all died."

When the old woman said, "They all died," her voice was strangely cheerful. Sakiko couldn't see the expression in her eyes behind her glasses. This side of the old woman's house faced north, and Sakiko sometimes heard the sound of birds twittering on the other side of her home. Apparently the woman kept the birdcages on the south side of the veranda, where it was sunny.

"They died? All of them?" Sakiko was rather bewildered. She cupped both hands around her mouth in trumpet fashion so that her voice would carry, and asked that.

"Indeed they did." Oddly enough, the old woman's whole face lit up in a smile as she replied. Then she hurried off, taking the birdcage with her. Sakiko saw her turn down the corridor that led to the south side of her home.

Sakiko ate breakfast and then she left the house, with no particular plan in mind. On her days off, she usually spent the mornings strolling and shopping. She walked along the hedge in front of the house next door, then along the wire mesh fence of the elementary school. She came upon three housewives in the neighborhood who were standing together and chatting.

"It's irritating, isn't it? To be kept waiting like this."

"Kept waiting?"

"By this fine weather. And by the criminal, too."

"But you say, 'waiting.'"

"Everyone is waiting for it to rain."

"It's the same thing day in and day out."

"Why doesn't it rain?"

"Who knows? Not me. They say the whole world is experiencing abnormal weather."

"Oh, for a drop of rain!"

"Maybe tonight. Anyway, the arsonist always strikes twice in the same place."

"The fair weather and the arsonist seem to be in cahoots."

"There's a breeze today. When there's a breeze, I get nervous."

"According to the police officer, first it's the gym, and next he targets the classroom building. With this wind, the fire will spread from the school to the mountains."

"There's no telling whether it will happen during the day or at night."

"On Sunday there's no one around, so today there's a big danger during the day."

Ordinarily, Sakiko didn't have the slightest interest in the housewives' conversations, but today, only because this one concerned

the fire, she was drawn in. She just stood listening, without partic-
ipating. When one of the women bowed to her she felt a bit guilty,
and she quickly walked away.

She boarded a bus and got off in front of the train station. In
contrast to the residential area, which was tightly girded by the surrounding mountains, here the sky spread out boundlessly. The
morning sky was like a tautly stretched, seamless blue expanse.
There was no haze, so the blue was unmarred. The crisp cold and
that pure blue were well matched. When the sky was this blue day
in and day out, she began to sense that behind it a drum was
pounding and an invisible festival was in full swing.

"I'm so thirsty," she murmured. In the middle of winter, in this
freezing cold, she felt thirsty. Gazing at the changeless, clear sky
made her thirsty.

"You came, after all," said a man's voice.

"After all?" said Sakiko, looking up to see that same investigator
descending the wide white staircase. She was at the police station.

"You're mean. Even though you have information, you hide it
and dole it out a bit at a time. You know something about a person
who might be the arsonist, don't you?"

The man motioned her to come up. He seemed to be order-
ing her.

Yes, of course I know, Sakiko said to herself.

She was hesitant, but she wanted to know more about the arsonist, so she began climbing the stairs. This building, which had
just been remodeled, was completely white and smooth. The room
to which the man escorted her didn't seem like a room for interro-
gation. A sign that read VISITOR'S ROOM #3 hung at its entrance.

"Please tell me anything you know. As I said the other day, I
guarantee that it won't cause trouble for you," said the officer, deliberately softening his facial expression.

Sakiko sat facing him across the table.

"I'd like you to explain in detail from the beginning."

Sakiko looked directly into the man's eyes, aware that her own eyes were gleaming.

The man began smoking a cigarette.

Sakiko initiated the discussion. "Did you say that both the first and the second incidents were at elementary schools? Naturally, the third one will be, too."

"Apparently he came by bicycle. Afterward we learned that just before the fire someone saw a bicycle parked nearby, both the first time and the second time."

"I might have known."

"What do you mean?"

"The evidence was a bicycle and a pocket flask of whiskey, right?" Sakiko continued. She remembered that there was a bicycle in the shed at her landlord's home. She remembered that in the garbage pile in the backyard were empty pocket flasks of the whiskey that her landlord was always drinking.

"That night. . . . I mean, what was the date?" Sakiko stammered.

"The first incident was the night of January 29, at ten o'clock."

"That night I was at home, but the landlord was away, and no one knew that I was there."

"You say strange things. This is no time for jokes." The officer stared blankly at her.

"The second incident was during the day, wasn't it. By chance, was it Saturday?"

"That's right. It was Saturday, February 3, at eleven in the morning."

"This is bad."

"What's the matter?"

"I don't work on Saturdays. If I'd gone to work, I wouldn't have had time to go to the elementary school. But it was a holiday, so I was at home. No one can vouch that I didn't set foot outside. The landlord and his wife were away for two weeks."

"Your name is Namioka, isn't it?" The officer leaned forward a bit and looked straight at her.

"No, it's Yamakawa. Yamakawa Sakiko."

"Do you know Public School Number 1 in the next town?"

"Yes, because an acquaintance of mine lives near there. It's the wooden building near the river, isn't it?"

"And of course you know R Elementary School on the outskirts of town, don't you?"

"It's odd—the schools that were set on fire are all ones that I know."

A sudden silence fell between them. The sound of a clock's second hand became audible. Sakiko glanced around the room. There was no clock anywhere. Somewhere in space a clock was ticking off the seconds. Tick-tock, tick-tock, went the methodical tapping, waiting for an explanation. Eventually, everything would surely be revealed. The arsonist's identity would surely be revealed.

"The first incident was at night, the second during the day. It seems that little by little the arsonist became greedy," said Sakiko, in a daze.

"Why do you say that?"

"First she just enjoyed the sight of the flames rising into the darkness. Because that in itself is beautiful."

"But then?" the officer urged.

Sakiko felt a pain in her chest, as if she were about to cough up blood.

"The criminal's interest shifted from a night fire to a day fire. Oh, that's because of the children."

"What about the children?"

Sakiko thought of those youngsters, the elementary school pupils, especially those in the lower grades, with their soft, plump bodies, who could do nothing for themselves but squeal. The arsonist had wanted to burn those little children to death. The little children packed into the classrooms would be roasted alive. Not in an instant, but slowly, slowly, enveloped in flames, enveloped in smoke, shrieking like locusts, they would burn on and on.

"The arsonist is definitely a woman!"

"Why did the person set the fires?" The change in the investigator's tone of voice roused Sakiko slightly from her fantasies.

"Who? That woman?"

"No one has said it was a woman."

I did it. Sakiko tried saying these words to herself. She felt something like red-hot iron pass through her throat and descend to the center of her body.

"May I have a glass of water?" asked Sakiko. She felt as if she'd forgotten where she was.

The policeman got up and went out. An empty reception room; new, smooth walls; a steel table; an imitation leather sofa; and an armchair—this was all that was here. Sakiko squinted her eyes. Her gaze passed through those things and peered into her interior. Was it her heartbeat that was throbbing so loudly inside her?

The investigator appeared, holding a cup of water in his hand.

"When you have nothing but good weather like this, you get thirsty," said Sakiko, and she drank the water in one gulp. "It's strange, isn't it. Even though it's cold, when the weather is fair day after day, I guess even your throat gets parched." Sakiko rambled on to the man, who stared at her without saying anything.

I did it. Sakiko tried saying the words again to herself. There was nothing to prove that she hadn't done it. There was a bicycle. There were empty whiskey bottles. And there was oil for an oil heater.

SAKIKO WAS GAZING DOWN on the city at night. She had ensconced herself in a seat by the window on the second floor of this coffee shop, and she was staring at the entrance to the department store across the street. The entire window was a single pane of glass, and the buses, taxis, and pedestrians passing by on the boulevard were clearly visible. The glass was thick, so no noise from outside was audible.

When she saw the man at the entrance to the department store across the street, Sakiko became excited. They had a date to meet there at 5:30. It was now 5:25. It wasn't completely dark outside yet, and the neon lights looked odd. The man was standing erectly, fully illuminated by the electric light at the department store entrance. He was facing the direction from which he thought Sakiko might appear—in other words, facing the spot where Sakiko was sitting—and moving his gaze back and forth. Because the lamp in the ceiling of that entryway was also turned on, Sakiko could see the man's every move as clearly as if he were bathed in a spotlight on stage. His handsome forehead, with its slightly receding hairline, glistened whitely, and his trenchcoat-style overcoat was attractive on his tall frame. The man glanced at his watch. Simultaneously, Sakiko glanced at her watch. It was 5:38. How many minutes? How many minutes between 10 and 20? How many tens of minutes? How long could this man wait?

Keeping her gaze fastened on the man, Sakiko recalled the conversation that she'd had with him earlier that day.

"Did you read in the newspaper about the smallpox incident?" she had asked the man during their lunch break. They both worked at the same company. According to the morning newspaper, it had been confirmed that a person who had just returned from a trip to India had contracted smallpox there.

A public-service-announcement vehicle from the civic center drove around the chilly, dark neighborhoods, urging residents through a loudspeaker to go to their community center to be vaccinated. Panicky citizens. Lines at the community center lasting until late at night. Mothers carrying babies. Young people leading grannies by the hand. Droves of people who had just thrown on a coat and rushed down. An antiseptic odor permeating the cavernous hall. Here and there groups of people clustered around city workers and nurses wearing white gowns and masks. Young mothers asking, "Are you inoculating even tiny babies like this?" Old men asking, "Do you have enough vaccine?" Everyone looking reassured to hear the serene voices of the nurses saying, "It's all right. Everyone just calm down."

"I'm glad it's not my *neighborhood. Probably everyone feels the same way—I'm so glad it didn't happen near* my *home,"* the man had said. He'd been standing in a sunny spot beside the vent on the roof.

"I don't feel that way," Sakiko had said, smiling faintly.

"What? You don't mind if you get smallpox?"

"I wonder why they're all in such a panic?"

She had recalled the photograph in the newspaper. It was a large photo showing mothers with determined expressions on their faces, babies and young children in tow. The women were baring their fleshy shoulders in order to get inoculated as quickly as possible.

"They looked as if they were screaming desperately, 'I don't want to die! I don't want to die!'"

"I guess it's better not to get smallpox than to get it."

"What annoys me is why no one seems to think, 'my life isn't worth a fig.' It's because they don't feel that way that they rush to be inoculated with that resolute look on their faces. I can't stand such mobs."

"Then why do you go on living?" he asked.

"Because I have no reason to die."

"That's a rash thing to say."

"But really, that's the most honest reply—for me."

"Can I see you tonight?" the man had asked at that point. This was always where her conversations with men led. The more outrageous her remarks, the more avidly men pursued her.

Through the window of the coffee shop, Sakiko continued to keep her gaze riveted on the man who stood waiting for her at the entrance of the department store. He glanced at his watch. At the same time, Sakiko glanced at her watch. It was already 5:52. It was 22 minutes past their appointment time. The man seemed to be getting a bit irritated. Over and over, he fretfully plunged his hands into his coat pockets, quickly shifted the direction of his gaze, and so on. Suddenly he spun around and disappeared into the department store. Right past the entrance was the counter for women's accessories. Maybe he thought that Sakiko might be shopping for something there. The man's upper body was cut off from Sakiko's view, but she could see his chocolate brown shoes, gleaming under the light inside the store. They didn't budge for several minutes. Finally the man came out to the entrance again. Two weeks earlier, Sakiko had made this kind of date with a different man. That man had stood at their meeting place for 32 minutes. Did her date for tonight have more perseverance?

Sakiko was assessing that. Actually, Sakiko was inordinately interested in observing men in this way. How much more exciting this sort of encounter was to her than actually meeting a man and conversing with him! She wished that she could go so far as to gaze at a man through binoculars. Would she play this kind of game with several more men? She knew all too well that before long she would lose interest in it.

"Excuse me, Miss. Would you mind sharing your table?" the waiter said. After finishing her coffee, Sakiko had continued to sit staring out of the window for over thirty minutes. Evidently the waiter was urging her to leave.

Sakiko didn't answer, but a young couple sat down across from her. The girl sat beside the window, so she was facing Sakiko directly. If Sakiko got up and left, the man would probably move to where she was now sitting, so that he and the girl could sit facing each other. Maybe it was Sakiko's imagination, but the pair seemed to be glancing hostilely at her, since she gave no sign of budging.

"Oh, that table is free," said the man, craning his neck.

At a table on the other side of the room, a party of four was standing up and preparing to leave.

"Oh no, someone else took it!" wailed the girl in a high-pitched, cloying voice.

Another party immediately slid into the empty seats. The faces of the young man and woman sitting across from her turned toward Sakiko and glared reprovingly, as if that was her fault.

Sakiko resumed looking at the department store entrance, from which she'd been distracted for a while. Her date was still standing there. The man came out to the sidewalk and looked up at the sky.

He seemed to be surveying it for signs of rain, but tonight there was none.

Suddenly Sakiko was seized by a strange notion. She felt as if the reproving stares being directed at her by the young couple who had happened to sit down across from her were actually being directed at her by the man with whom she had a date. That man had taken possession of the eyes of the couple in front of her and was now glowering at Sakiko. And another image was superimposed on that one: the menacing looks that investigator had given her.

The imaginary arson, with its vivid flames and smoke and children's screams, resumed its part-painful, part-pleasurable burning inside her. The fire had been on Thursday night. On Friday evening she'd met with the police officer, and on Saturday and Sunday during the day she'd gone again to meet with him. Today was Monday, and the case had not yet been solved.

Sakiko reflected with dismay on what she'd done the night before. Five or six empty pocket flasks of whiskey that the landlord was always drinking and throwing out had been lying on the garbage heap in the backyard. Late last night she'd taken one of those and filled it with the oil used in the oil heater. Ordinarily, if she didn't wear a coat she'd catch cold, but last night she was oblivious to the chill in the outdoor air. As she held the bottle filled with oil in her hand, she felt as if she were clenching burning coals. The throbbing of an ominous drum seemed to be coming from somewhere deep inside her and reverberating infinitely through space. She corked the bottle and placed it in the dark garden. When she took two or three steps backward she could no longer see it. But she was acutely aware of something ghastly, lurking deep in the darkness, like a newborn infant that had just begun to breathe.

She took two or three steps and looked back. "Now there's evidence," she whispered.

For some reason, she'd felt relieved. She had returned to her room and fallen into a sound sleep.

The young couple sitting across from Sakiko must have moved to another table; they had disappeared. Sakiko glanced through the window at the department store entrance. Her date was still waiting there.

SAKIKO WALKED OUT into the morning air just after seven o'-clock, as usual. Today the skies were fair again. The smooth blue sky that stretched overhead was unmarred by a single cloud. The mountains loomed over this side of the street, where the house in which she lived, the house next door, and the elementary school stood in a row. The grass close to the earth was completely dried out and had turned slightly whitish. That color and the blue sky made a striking contrast.

Everyone was waiting for rain, parched with thirst. It just won't rain, will it? Oh, for a drop of rain! Even though it's this cold, doesn't your throat feel dry? Why is this lasting so long? Strange that a blue sky should seem so ominous. Something's about to happen, there's no doubt about it, it's ready to happen, something. . . .

During this monotonous stretch of fair weather, suddenly an arsonist appears on the scene. She's not a shifty or a vicious type of individual. From a sky so blue that it seems to have been created with undiluted, bright-blue oil paint, a single desire emerges, as if cut out with scissors from that pure blue sky. And that desire begins to pervade the entire world. The culprit steals into the midst of the people who are waiting day after day for a rainfall. She blends in with those people. At the slightest provocation, she leaps out of their midst and executes the deed. But the culprit is nowhere to be found.

As Sakiko was on her way to work, she saw the investigator walking toward her. She walked straight toward him, smiling thinly. Why bother to use a lie detector? If she were subjected to a lie detector test, she'd surely respond the same way as the criminal, she thought.

She walked alongside her next-door neighbor's hedge. The blue sky was growing brighter by the moment; it was definitely developing into a fine day. Whether the old woman was still snug in her bed or had already gone out somewhere, her house was shrouded in silence and darkness. Sakiko heard an intermittent muffled sound, as if a cough was being stifled, coming from the veranda on the south side of that house. It sounded like the old woman's cough. Suddenly there was a voice.

"I set the fires! I set the fires!"

It was that mynah bird talking. The voice resembled the old woman's, but it was slightly different from the shrill voice in which she chatted with people. It was a mumbling voice, as when she was talking to herself.

Spirited laughter welled up in Sakiko's throat. The distance between her and the investigator was shrinking.

"You're out working bright and early today, too," said Sakiko, deliberately trying to aggravate the man's suspicions about her.

"Keeping tabs on things is my job," he replied, as he approached her.

"'Keeping tabs'? Things already seem to be out of your control," said Sakiko, nodding toward the house next door. But the voice was silent. Only a noise that resembled stifled coughing was audible.

"Why is that?" the man asked, coming to an abrupt halt.

Sakiko resisted the urge to reply to that question. She felt like saying, "Because not only I but the old woman next door has begun to go mad."

The Oracle

Last night Yōko dreamed about her late husband.

The dream went like this. She was beside a swimming pool, hurrying after Gōkichi, when he turned around and looked at her with a gloomy expression on his face that she'd never once seen while he was alive. Then he kept on leisurely striding away from her. Why was he making such a face? Bewildered, Yōko stood stock-still. Their married life had been brief, but in those three years Gōkichi had never once looked cross. The sight of his gloomy face stirred up something gloomy in her, too. That feeling intensified by the moment. An ominous shadow seemed to steal across the sparkling white pool deck. Overly bright light poured from the ocean and sky onto this hotel towering above the seashore. It rebounded off the stark white walls, which were tossing up a constant spray of light. But Yōko felt the shadow that had just crept into the scene begin to deepen and spread across the beach overflowing with light and heat. It seemed to be summer, because although she herself was fully clothed, Gōkichi, who was walking away from her along the poolside, was wearing only a pair of swimming trunks. That muscular body, well toned from years of playing tennis, was receding into the distance, its back to her. Judging from the sprightliness that she detected in his step, the look on his face moments before must have been one of rejection, as if he considered Yōko a nuisance. There was no one around. The pool itself was empty. Had the water dried up during a long hot spell? Something like slime was stuck to the bottom of the pool, like a dry membrane, and that crisp substance was full of cracks. Yōko held up her hand to shade her eyes. Everything was dazzlingly bright, so she did that to help her see. Gōkichi kept walking away from her, and at the middle of the pool he descended a metal ladder to the bottom. Then again he began walking away, across the concrete pool bottom. Strangely enough, at the far end of the pool there were five showers lined up at regular intervals. Water was cascading, like a white waterfall, from the one in the center. Yōko thought that Gōkichi was going to take a shower there, and she stared straight at it. Just then, from within that white waterfall, a woman's naked arm suddenly emerged and beckoned to Gōkichi. As if irritated by his leisurely approach, the arm stretched out even farther. The gesture made the woman reveal a glimpse of herself. Yōko's heart gave one strong thud. The woman was Gōkichi's older sister, Haruyo. She was wearing a navy blue bathing suit; the color made her white skin look all the whiter. Because of the distance between them Yōko couldn't make out Haruyo very clearly. But she could see her look at Gōkichi and beam, emitting a gleam of light like a camera flash. Yōko watched, stunned, as at the far edge of her field of vision, Haruyo lured Gōkichi into the white waterfall and the pair vanished from sight. The midsummer light at the seashore was overly bright. But at the center of any overly bright light, countless flecks of darkness flicker. When Yōko stared at those dark motes, they gradually dissolved into blackness, a blackness that steadily deepened. And yet, how dazzlingly bright it was! Yōko shielded her eyes with her hand and continued to gaze intently in the direction of the scene that she'd just witnessed.

After awakening, Yōko kept wondering why she had dreamed such a thing.

While musing about this and that, she recalled that some time ago she'd had a dream about Haruyo and Gōkichi, but she didn't remember anything about it. The only thing she was sure of was that the woman had been Haruyo. Perhaps because she'd forgotten it, that dream did not distress her now. But the strange thing was, why should she dream about Haruyo and Gōkichi twice? In their three years of married life, Yōko had never once harbored suspicions about that sort of thing—that is, about Gōkichi's relationships with women. In the first place, Gōkichi had been a husband who was so sweet and so considerate in every way. Had that extraordinary sweetness been a kind of mask?

Lying face up on her bed, Yōko surrendered to such ruminations. Someone was walking down the concrete hallway on the other side of the wall, footsteps tapping in a regular rhythm. The room that Yōko used as a bedroom was on the north side of the apartment complex. Since Gōkichi had died, she'd gotten in the habit of sleeping late in the morning. She slept right beside the outside corridor, so the sound of footsteps passed right beside her head, one set after another. Especially on mornings like this, when she was plunged in certain reflections, she felt as if people were trampling across the intimate thoughts that radiated in all directions from her head to the outside world.

Yōko glanced at her clock and saw that it was before nine. She left the dark bedroom that had only one small window, went out to the dining area, which faced south, and opened the curtain. The sunlight had grown more intense with the passage of spring, and it was flickering across the leaves of the plants on the veranda. On the roof of the apartment building next door, the laundry hung out by the housewives who had risen early was fluttering in the breeze. Its whiteness, reflecting the morning sun, came piercingly to her eyes.

But more keenly than this actual sunlight, Yōko was aware of the suffocating sunlight that suffused the midsummer beach in her dream. It seemed to still be clinging to her. She felt as if she were now standing on that midsummer beach and picturing the plants and laundry, glistening in spring sunlight, at this apartment complex.

She wanted to quickly resume her usual morning routine, so she took a few steps across the dining area. But those steps, and the act of washing her face at the sink toward which she was now walking, for some reason seemed like a sham. She stopped and stood beside the dining table, vaguely wondering if there was now one single deed that wasn't a sham.

Be that as it might, why had Gōkichi and his sister Haruyo appeared that way in her dream? In the dream, the two of them had been enveloped in a very voluptuous atmosphere. Moreover, something dazzling that looked as if it would burn to the touch surrounded them, and the pair had vanished into the center of that aura.

Now Yōko was staring at that scene, and at the same time she was glancing at the telephone on the table. She was shifting her gaze back and forth between the scene at the pool beside the beach and the phone receiver. It seemed as if that distant scene and this object here in front of her existed on the same plane.

Yōko picked up the phone receiver. She knew that in her present state of mind this was the only deed that wasn't a sham. She flipped through her address book with her right hand. Although the time it took didn't seem long to her, apparently it was too long, and the warning signal began to beep. Yōko replaced the receiver. The beeping seemed to continue, as if urging her to do something. What was it telling her to do? Hurry up and dial! Or else, Don't do something so foolish!

When Yōko found the phone number, she ended up dialing.

The phone rang for a long time. She wondered if they were out already, even though it was still around nine o'clock. She waited patiently.

"Hello," said a high-pitched voice, panting breathlessly.

"Haruyo? Is that you, Haruyo?" said Yōko, unsure of whose voice it was.

"She can't come now. She called a cab. We're waiting in front of the gate. We heard the phone ring, so I came in," said the girl, who was in kindergarten. Apparently she wasn't going to school today.

"I was thinking of visiting her today. It's Yōko. Tell her that."

What in the world did she intend to do when she met Haruyo? Yōko asked herself. But no matter what she did, she had to meet her. The urgency of that was transmitted, like a tingling electric current, from the atmosphere of the dream all the way to Yōko, who was awake and standing here talking.

"She won't be home during the day. Come tonight." The precocious child spoke in a tone of voice that was exactly like Haruyo's.

"Where's Mama going?" Yōko asked. She suddenly imagined Haruyo's destination to be that hotel with a pool by the midsummer seashore.

"We're all going to Grandma's house. Well, see you later. The taxi's waiting." The girl slammed the receiver down.

That rejecting sound, although produced by a young child's innocent action, exacerbated Yōko's uneasiness.

Yōko washed her face and ate breakfast.

I know—I'll go too, it suddenly occurred to her. Haruyo and her children were on their way to the house where Gōkichi's mother lived alone. Since Gōkichi had died ten months before, Yōko's living expenses, for one thing, were a matter of concern. Yōko had to make a decision about her future soon. She'd been just about to go consult with her mother-in-law about possibly returning to her family home and getting a job.

Yōko thought that she would spend some time at the department store shopping for a small gift and arrive there just after noon. Since she was the type to act on impulse, she quickly changed her clothes. She closed the window and drew the curtains. She stood in the front hallway and looked back at the apartment. In the faint light that filtered evenly through the sheer curtains, the household objects looked as if they were floating there languidly and forlornly. Because Yōko's married life had lasted only three years, this place wasn't yet stuffed with things, and it would be a long time before those objects would darken with the humidity. The stereo, the table and chairs, the chest of drawers, the china cabinet, the mirror, the pictures—they were all only three years old, and somehow they didn't quite seem real yet.

"Don't seem real," Yōko murmured.

When she said this, Gōkichi, whom she had trusted implicitly, for some reason began to seem unreal. She was able to feel this way because the events of last night's dream seemed very real. The dream she'd had a while ago, which she couldn't remember clearly, reinforced that feeling.

Yōko left her apartment. Everywhere was suffused with unexpectedly radiant spring sunshine. Slivers of sunlight seemed to be glinting in the wind, and the air was filled with the sense of liberation that early April typically brings. But today, Yōko's spirits weren't uplifted by the fine weather.

What exactly was the happiness that she was so sure she'd obtained from her relationship with Gōkichi? Yōko wondered. The one who had been entirely responsible for that was Gōkichi; after all, he was six years older than she. If there'd been something false about that happiness, it surely would have come to light sometime. But Gōkichi had died suddenly, leaving behind three years of mostly rose-colored memories, so now there was no way of verifying what the essence of that happiness had been.

At the department store, Yōko bought some Japanese cakes for her mother-in-law and ate an early lunch. The atmosphere of her dream hadn't yet dissipated; it clung tenaciously to her. She knew from past experience that a dream would haunt her for no more than a day. Last night was the first time that she'd had a dream of that kind, but there were dozens of times when she'd had an absurd dream that nevertheless had a vivid sense of reality and hovered around her. It would linger throughout the following day, but by the day after that, it would have evaporated. Why a dream only survived for one day was a mystery to her. At any rate, if she could just put up with it all day today, last night's dream ought mercifully to vanish. But Yōko felt that she absolutely had to meet with Haruyo before the dream dissolved. Probably this was because she wanted to find out something about Gōkichi, and she thought the meeting might provide her with a clue.

Yōko walked past a movie theater where there was an advertising poster painted in garish colors hanging in the entrance. She immediately averted her eyes. The poster depicted a man whose body was tilted diagonally forward, his face twisted in an expression of agony. Fresh blood was dripping from his mouth and forehead. Behind him stood another man with both arms widely outstretched; his purplish face wore a look of either alarm or terror. Someone had shot the man in front with a pistol. It was probably a scene from a gangster movie.

Yōko had been quite fond of going with Gōkichi to see gangster movies, but since he had died in a traffic accident, she couldn't stand the sight of blood. She hadn't witnessed the accident. When she saw Gōkichi he had already been cleaned up. But the wounds that remained here and there on his face, which had become like white wax, made Yōko imagine what she hadn't actually seen. On top of that, all the bones on the ten fingers of both hands had been broken, so his hands couldn't even be clasped together in a reverent gesture.

The train ride to the small city where her mother-in-law lived took nearly an hour. During the entire time, Yōko was, as usual, absorbed in thoughts of Gōkichi.

She tried picturing his facial features. There was a hint of occidental blood in them. Perhaps it was because the contours of his features—such as his prominent nose and deep-set eyes—were well defined, and his head was relatively small in proportion to his body. Although he looked vaguely western, his complexion was rather dark, so one imagined the area of the West that was close to Asia. People often used to make such remarks to him, half jokingly. He worked for a trading company, and the courteous manner typical of employees of trading companies extended even to his relationship with Yōko. He seemed like a nearly perfect husband.

Had that been a mask? Yōko continued to wonder about that.

Why had Gōkichi and his sister Haruyo suddenly appeared, as if to wantonly destroy the memory of picture-perfect happiness that Yōko cherished?

Yōko got off the train and boarded a bus. The trip from her apartment to her mother-in-law's home took a full two hours. She looked at her watch and saw that it was a little before one o'clock. It was the perfect time for a visit. She got off the bus and walked along the main thoroughfare. Dust and exhaust blew into her slightly perspiring face and clung to it, just as in the city. But when she turned down a side street, the air filled her lungs completely like pure water. It was redolent of flowers. Ahead of her she saw a large house with a white wooden fence where cherry trees were in full bloom. She eagerly imbibed that fragrance, feeling as if her body were turning the pink color of the blossoms.

She passed an elementary school on her right. The wooden schoolhouse and the gymnasium that she'd seen there before were gone; perhaps they'd burned down in a fire, or they were being remodeled. In their place stood only iron scaffolding. The construction workers were apparently taking the day off, and classes were probably being held elsewhere. The entire school grounds were utterly silent, bathed in the kind of brilliant light that produces heat hazes.

The outer gate and the front door were always locked at her mother-in-law's home. Yōko would ring the bell at the gate over and over. A sound like birds twittering would come from the back of the spacious, Japanese-style home. Then Yōko would hear bustling, energetic footsteps—quite unlike those of a typical seventy-one-year-old—scurrying down a corridor. Next would come the sound of a key turning in the front door lock. Her mother-in-law's pure white hair would appear, an overly cordial voice would peal, "Oh, my goodness!" then the key in the gate would be turned and the gate opened. That was the usual sequence of events. But today Haruyo and her family were here. So perhaps because the old woman wasn't worried about burglars, Yōko was able to pass freely through both the gate and the front door.

"That's right! Let's try it once more," pealed her mother-in-law's shrill voice.

Yōko turned down the corridor that led to the south side of the home. That place, too, was permeated with the bright sunlight that produces heat waves, and heavy with the scent of light in a sun-drenched spot.

> Grandmama, young Grandmama,
> Young forevermore.
> Grandmama, pretty Grandmama,
> Pretty forevermore.

The two children were chanting the words in unison, like a song. Her mother-in-law's girlish laughter zigzagged up through the warm spring air.

Yōko stood there silently, her eyes riveted on the scene. Her mother-in-law sat in front of the alcove in the living room, her robust figure impeccably attired in a kimono. Haruyo's children behaved just as if they were performing the series of gestures set forth in the script of a kindergarten play. When they finished reciting their lines, the two joined hands and walked up to their grandmother, bowed deeply, then withdrew. Obviously her mother-in-law was making them do this. The old woman, who lived alone, sometimes came up with zany notions. Maybe living alone for a long time would drive a person mad, little by little. It occurred to Yōko that being manipulated by last night's dream into pursuing Haruyo all the way here was perhaps symptomatic of the same kind of madness.

"My goodness! How marvelous that all of you should come to visit me today!" effused her mother-in-law as she rose to greet Yōko. That four visitors should rush in to dispel the cloud of boredom that enveloped her day after day made the old woman as giddy as if a flock of sparrows had begun chirping inside her. The lenses of her silver-rimmed glasses twinkled, reflecting her delight.

"Where's Haruyo?" Yōko asked immediately.

"Mama's at the ocean," said the six-year-old girl who had answered Yōko's phone call earlier.

"Where at the ocean?" Yōko countered. Again, she felt that light at the midsummer seashore begin to veil her eyes.

"Mama's napping," added the four-year-old boy, as if competing with his sister.

"Come now, let's eat these yummy sweets that Yōko brought us." Yōko's mother-in-law went into the smaller room next door and began opening the package on the table.

"Isn't Haruyo here?" asked Yōko again, directing the question to the old woman.

"She said that she came here because she wanted to see the ocean. But she changed her mind and I guess she's taking a nap upstairs. She says the children are so noisy that she usually doesn't sleep well." Her mother-in-law clattered the dishes as she replied.

"I think I'll just go up and see," Yōko said, rising.

"Mama's a loonybird," said the girl.

"Mama's a liar," chimed the little boy, falteringly, right after her.

From the living room, her mother-in-law looked at Yōko, her eyes widening in a show of surprise at such remarks. At the same moment, Yōko looked at her. But the old woman's focus became somewhat vague and shifted toward the children.

"Who was that? Who said such a thing?" she said, feigning sternness.

The children looked at each other and giggled.

Yōko climbed the stairs and stood on the landing. The outdoor scene had a slightly greenish tinge, because the trees on the mountains that overlooked the garden were all sprouting new leaves.

"Are you resting?" Yōko called toward the bedroom.

"Who's that?" replied Haruyo's clear voice. It wasn't the voice of someone taking a nap.

"It's Yōko."

"Don't open the door! Wait a minute!" said Haruyo, sounding flustered.

Then Yōko could hear the sound of objects being picked up and put away. The sound of several sheets of thin paper being shuffled together; the sound of a chainlike object jingling; the sound of a heavy, round metal object plunking down on thick paper; the sound of a lid being hastily placed on a large pasteboard box. Then there was silence.

"Please come in," Haruyo said, this time pronouncing each syllable slowly and distinctly.

"You *weren't* napping, were you," said Yōko as she opened the sliding door. Then she entered the room, looking straight at Haruyo. The reflection from the garden pond was throwing rings of light on the ceiling. Perhaps because of that, the whole room was steeped in a pleasant languor. Yōko's head reeled, as though she'd suddenly plunged into a large whirlpool.

"Will you have one?" Haruyo held a pack of cigarettes out to Yōko. Yōko then noticed that in the ashtray there were already seven or eight butts from cigarettes that Haruyo had smoked.

Yōko hadn't seen Haruyo since way back, just after the various matters related to Gōkichi's funeral had all been settled. But

whenever she met Haruyo, who would thrust out a pack of cigarettes like a man, they would skip the usual formalities and begin
conversing in earnest. Even if the two of them hadn't met for a
long time, the intimacy that lingered from their previous encounter would immediately revive when they saw each other, and
they could slip right back into it. Haruyo had a way about her
that made this possible. Yōko's constant feeling that as a woman
she was no match for Haruyo was not only because Haruyo was
eight years her senior. That feeling would still have been one of
pure admiration, if only it weren't for last night's dream.

"Won't you smoke?" Haruyo was still holding out the pack of
cigarettes.

"I guess so." Yōko wasn't in the habit of smoking, but she took one.

Just then, as if it had been coiled up inside the cigarette, a scene
that she'd forgotten sprang to mind. Between the time that she'd
been introduced to Gōkichi and when they were married, Gōkichi
had once offered her a cigarette just like that.

"No thanks, I don't smoke," Yōko had replied. At that time,
there were still few women who smoked.

"Oh, don't you?" Gōkichi had made a face as if he realized his
mistake, and had withdrawn the pack.

Yōko now remembered thinking at the time that Gōkichi was
used to offering cigarettes to some woman who liked to smoke.
But that momentary anxiety was like a pebble that had simply
bounced past the sugarcoated relationship that Gōkichi had created for Yōko.

"So you went to see the ocean?" asked Yōko. She awkwardly inhaled the smoke, then hastily blew it out. She wasn't used to smoking, so she couldn't smoke elegantly like Haruyo.

"I suppose that's what the children said," said Haruyo, smiling a
bit wearily. When Haruyo smiled, her eyes seemed to emit a flash
of light. In Yōko's dream, that light had been a large white burst
that illuminated the entire poolside by the beach.

"Haruyo, do you know the ocean at Ōiso?"

"Of course. There isn't a place I don't know from here to the end of the Shōnan Coast."

"Do you know the Long Beach Hotel there?" Yōko felt as if she had come here today for the purpose of asking this question.

"You went there with Gōkichi, didn't you?" Haruyo answered, then she puffed quickly on her cigarette.

"How did you know?"

Yōko had gone there with Gōkichi the summer before last. She'd stood at the poolside that was the setting for her dream, and Gōkichi had swum alone. For some reason, from childhood, Yōko hadn't been able to swim. The sunlight, which seemed to be mixed with the salt that had evaporated from the ocean water, had gradually grown scorching, but Yōko wasn't even using a parasol. She stood motionless, with her eyes riveted on Gōkichi as he swam in the pool. On that occasion, why had she watched so anxiously, as if she feared that Gōkichi might disappear from sight? After all, it wasn't the ocean but a pool, so there was no chance of losing sight of him. And yet, even though she held her hand over her eyes to shield them from the dazzling brightness, the rings of light that rose constantly from the surface of the pool water blurred her vision.

"How?" repeated Yōko.

"Because we always went there in the summer."

"You and Gōkichi?"

"I think there were even times when just the two of us went."

"Really? I never knew that. Haruyo, did you and Gōkichi ever quarrel or anything?"

"What do you mean? It was a long period of time. I can't sum it up in a few words."

"Someone once said that when you and Gōkichi walked side by side you looked like lovers."

"Who said that? When?"

"Never mind. I just remembered something now. You know how sometimes you suddenly remember something that you'd completely forgotten?"

It was true. No one had ever said such a thing. But one day—this was also while she and Gōkichi were engaged—Yōko had seen Haruyo and Gōkichi walking side by side. On that occasion too, the image had been like a scrap of paper that had simply fluttered past the honey-sweet relationship that Gōkichi had created for Yōko's sake.

"So, what about the ocean?" This time Haruyo asked the question.

"It doesn't matter. Never mind." Yōko ground out her cigarette in the ashtray and got up. She realized that it was useless to continue this sort of conversation. When she thought about it, it seemed that trying to ferret meaning out of a dream was probably a bit crazy of her.

Yōko went to the window that faced north and looked outside. At the second-floor window of the house next door, a woman stood facing her direction and staring into space. Since the height and the wall location of the two windows were nearly identical, Yōko and the other woman were face to face with each other. Yōko wondered what the woman was thinking right then. Probably she wondered that because the woman appeared to be about the same age as herself, but also because there wasn't a trace of vitality about her. She gave the impression that standing there alone at that moment was the entire meaning of her existence. Whereas Yōko, under the influence of a dream, was full of turmoil, the woman across from her seemed like an empty shell, from either listlessness or boredom. It struck Yōko as somehow strange that she and a total stranger were facing each other in perfect alignment—Yōko at this window and the other woman at that one. Since no one was watching, what if she and that woman were to enter into a secret pact and trade destinies? Just as Yōko was thinking this, the other woman, who had been staring straight at her for a while, stopped that and withdrew from the window.

Grandmama, young Grandmama,
Young forevermore.
Grandmama, pretty Grandmama,
Pretty forevermore.

Yōko could hear the children's voices chanting the verse again downstairs. Then her mother-in-law's shrill laughter quickly rippled up.

"You know that Mother keeps birds, don't you?" When Haruyo said this, Yōko left the window and went back beside her.

"She bought a mynah bird, didn't she? And I heard that before that she had parakeets and finches and others. Mother said it's difficult to keep good birds. She said they usually die within a short time."

"That's not true. Mother kills them all."

"What!?" Yōko stared at Haruyo.

Perhaps because her eyes stung from the smoke she exhaled from her cigarette, Haruyo narrowed her large eyes, so she looked as if she were smiling.

"You didn't know? Gōkichi never told you?"

"Why does she kill them?"

"Father had affairs with one woman after another. Mother names the birds after those women and she kills them one after another, even now."

"Well! That's really something. She doesn't show that side of herself at all." Yōko pictured the polite, refined demeanor of the mother-in-law she knew. And yet, there was a hint of madness in her making her grandchildren sing such a song.

"That's Mother's vicious side, isn't it."

"But Gōkichi never said a word about such things. I wonder why," Yōko mused. The topic did nothing to improve her mood that day.

As Yōko had expected, the dream's spell lasted only a day.

But now that her mind was calm, she felt like taking the opportunity to examine closely her three years with Gōkichi. She began the process by sitting alone on the dining room sofa and picturing Gōkichi sitting directly opposite her.

"You look pale. Are you all right?" Gōkichi had asked Yōko one Sunday morning. He'd been reading a magazine, and the moment he looked up, he perceptively analyzed Yōko's facial expression. If Yōko showed signs of a cold or was short on sleep, usually it was Gōkichi who would call attention to a condition of which she herself had scarcely been aware. His way of immediately discerning subtle symptoms inside Yōko that she hadn't noticed and nursing her back to health reminded her of a mother's solicitude, or rather, of a father's thoughtfulness. That was it. Yōko had regarded Gōkichi with the same sense of dependency that one feels toward a mother or father.

It was Gōkichi who'd suggested that they fill the veranda with green plants. It was always Gōkichi who anticipated and verbalized Yōko's desires. So the two of them had gone every Sunday to this shop and that, buying one potted plant after another. Now there were twenty-eight plants thriving on the veranda, their leaves green and glossy. When it came to their apartment's decor, too, what Gōkichi suggested was always what Yōko was vaguely wishing for.

Everything had been that way.

The model husband, the kind of man desired by any ordinary married woman, was just this type. Moreover, what any ordinary married woman desired in a husband was to always know what her husband was doing. When Gōkichi was late to return home because his work or his tennis match had lasted longer than usual, he never failed to phone Yōko and let her know. When he was going on a business trip, he told Yōko which hotel he'd be staying at and what his work schedule would be. Yōko, who was at home, knew everything about Gōkichi, who was outside. More precisely, Gōkichi kept Yōko informed of everything.

Why had he been so perfect? Yōko wondered about this now.

It suddenly occurred to her that there was only one thing that Gōkichi never mentioned. It was the topic of women. In retrospect this seemed peculiar, but at the time, Yōko had been convinced that it was because Gōkichi had no interest in any woman beside herself. They'd married when Gōkichi was thirty years old. What in the world had such an eligible man been doing until the age of thirty?

While she was pondering such matters, Yōko again dreamed of Gōkichi and a woman. The woman wasn't Haruyo. But the expression on Gōkichi's face at the beginning of the dream was nearly the same as it had been in the dream in which Haruyo appeared.

Gōkichi turned around. He looked at Yōko, who was approaching him, with a scowl on his face that she'd never seen while he was alive. Astonished, Yōko stood stock-still in the middle of the road. Gōkichi turned down an alley where a cinder block wall stretched on the right. That scowl seemed to mean, don't come after me. But Yōko couldn't restrain herself from following him. Suddenly twilight began to spread through the sky. The cinder block wall ended at the cul-de-sac of the alley. A little bungalow, like a rental home, stood there. The house had no front yard or anything; the sliding door leading to its front hall was flush with the alley. It was a very poor-looking home, but it blazed with almost overly bright lighting, as if waiting to welcome a great crowd of guests. It must have seemed overly bright because evidently every light in it was turned on, including even the bathroom light and the desk lamps. Yōko realized that she'd never before seen a home in which every single light was on. The house seemed to be shining of its own accord because of that absurd lighting. Yōko opened the front door, not knowing what to expect. She was confronted with the scene of a happy family. Of course, the living room, too, was a blaze of intense light, as if a spotlight were being directed at it from somewhere. A man and a woman and a boy of around six years old were there. The man was Gōkichi. The woman appeared to be slightly older than Yōko. She wasn't girlish like Yōko; rather, she had an air of serenity. She wasn't a pretty woman, but she had an individuality about her, so you wouldn't forget her after seeing her once. Above all, she looked very happy. Yōko stood in the front hallway, dumbfounded. But no one noticed her. She called out to Gōkichi, but it seemed as if her voice didn't carry; no one looked in her direction. She called out twice, three times.

Upon awakening Yōko realized that she'd seen that woman someplace before. The woman's facial characteristics were still vivid in her mind. Her eyebrows were thick and she had a well-shaped mouth. When she looked up, her right eye became slightly larger than her left eye. She had a fair complexion. That was especially striking because she'd been standing beside the dark-skinned Gōkichi. She was of average weight and height.

Even though Yōko remembered her appearance in such minute detail, she had no idea who the woman could be. Her dream the other day had affected her in the same way. It was really hard to resist the spellbinding power of a dream. When she moved her hands to get something or moved her legs to cross the room, the dream clung tenaciously to her. It invaded her living space. With every breath she took, the dream murmured. Being held captive like this by a dream was suffocating; Yōko began to feel that this might be the same sensation that the mentally ill constantly experience. Her real life became utterly debilitated, while the life of her dream, a mere phantom, pulsated with vitality.

Yōko thought she would take a walk, in order to escape from the situation. The wind was blowing. The moment she stepped outside the door, something came to her. The woman in her dream was the clerk at the necktie counter in the department store. The reason Yōko hadn't been able to recall that for the life of her was that the woman in the dream had radiated a wifely placidity that the woman herself was entirely lacking. Anyway, Yōko would go to the department store and have a look.

Even though it was mid-April, the wind was chilly. Each time it blew gustily, dust sprayed up from the ground. Then a scene that was as vivid as a photo emerged from deep inside Yōko. The incident had seemed trivial when it occurred, so why had it now assumed significance? She had felt vaguely disturbed by it, but it had whizzed through her consciousness and descended into her subconscious. Had it now surfaced, together with the meaning that at the time she had only dimly perceived?

It had happened at the necktie counter, about a year before.

"I think this is very attractive on you," the woman had said to Gōkichi.

"You sure know what a person likes," Gōkichi had replied.

"Everyone is nice enough to tell me that." The woman had lowered her eyes a bit, so the thickness of her eyebrows was very apparent.

"How many dozens of customers do you wait on in a day?" Gōkichi had asked her. Yōko, who was standing close by, had thought that it was an awfully chummy way of speaking to a stranger. By "customers," he must have meant male customers.

"Oh my, it's quite all right," said the woman, laughing.

In retrospect, it was a peculiar conversation. What in the world was "Oh my, it's quite all right" supposed to mean? Yōko wondered. Should she take it as merely a female clerk's frivolous response to a male customer's banter?

It took only twenty minutes by subway to get to the department store.

The first-floor necktie counter had changed locations from a year before, and Yōko didn't see that woman.

"A person with thick eyebrows, whose right eye becomes slightly bigger than her left eye," said Yōko to the clerk at the new necktie counter. She was so completely under the spell of the dream that asking herself why she was doing such an odd thing was powerless to restrain her.

"I wonder if she means Miss Nozawa?" whispered that saleswoman to another one.

"Just a moment, please," the first saleswoman said, and she walked away. Yōko could see her dark, navy blue uniform as she passed one sales counter after another.

Suddenly Yōko felt anxious. If the saleswoman returned with the woman in her dream, what would she do? She realized that she was behaving this way despite the fact that she didn't have the slightest belief in things that appeared in her dreams. But if the dream turned out to be reality, how in the world should she and that woman deal with each other?

Yōko stepped back and hid herself behind a large pillar.

The same saleswoman came back alone. Even so, Yōko thought that the woman might follow a bit later, so for a while she didn't budge. But the woman did not appear. When Yōko finally went over to the necktie counter, the clerk assumed a professional, affable manner and said, "She's working at a different counter. We don't know right now which one it is."

As she listened to the clerk's unctuous voice, Yōko stared absentmindedly at the cuff links that were set here and there among the neckties in the glass case. "But she *is* here in the store, is she?" she asked, feeling as if it didn't even matter to her anymore.

"Yes. I'm terribly sorry," said the saleswoman politely.

Suddenly, something occurred to Yōko. "That's amber, isn't it?" she asked, pointing to a certain pair of cuff links in the glass case. Gōkichi had owned a very similar pair.

"Yes. That item is an original of our store. Would you like to see it?"

The clerk took the pair out. Yōko placed them on her hand and saw that the translucent golden stones had twelve faces. Each cuff link consisted of two such stones whose bottom surfaces were joined by a platinum chain. There was a platinum bead ornament where the chain connected to each base. The longer she looked at the cuff links, the more they seemed like Gōkichi's.

"They're only sold at this store?"

"Yes. They're a bit expensive, but the beauty of the design is unique."

"Have you just begun selling them recently?"

"We've had them for about a year."

It was the cuff links that made Yōko want to hunt for the woman named Nozawa who was somewhere here in this department store. It was indeed about a year before that Gōkichi had received the cuff links—from an acquaintance, he had said. Even though it was certainly feasible that the acquaintance had purchased the item at this store, Yōko felt that she absolutely must meet the Nozawa woman. But how in the world should she go around, from counter to counter, in a twelve-story department store? Images of each actual counter surged, one by one, into her mental blueprint of the store, and that alone made her head spin.

She decided to start on the eighth floor, because for some reason it seemed that the Furniture and Tableware Department was a likely place to find the Nozawa woman. When she stepped off the elevator, her eyes were dazzled by gaudy hues of red, yellow, green, and blue. Plastic cups, large bowls, small bowls, dishes, flowerpots, and so forth, cute as toys, were neatly arranged on shelf after shelf. That cuteness was an artificial quality. Although it was tableware, each piece seemed like an independent object, having no practical function, that gleamed brightly with its own life. That was because its color looked like paint straight from the tube. Yōko had never experienced such a sensation in a department store. Perhaps today she was tired. She felt that she simply could not bring herself to enter the rows of shelves laden with countless plastic dishes, so she went toward the chinaware. There too, what confronted her was nothing but pieces of glass, rather than tableware. The surfaces of cut glass twinkled under the fluorescent lights in the ceiling, and they all seemed to be winking at her at once. If she looked closely she could distinguish cups, sugar bowls, ashtrays, candy dishes, ice buckets, glasses, and so forth, but if she stared even harder, the objects disintegrated into pieces of glass, and all those individual glass fragments were teeming around, each brimming with its own life.

So many things are closing in on me, thought Yōko as she stared vacantly across the department. The saleswomen standing around all looked like the Nozawa woman.

Yōko headed for the furniture section. The first thing she came to was a corner crammed with china cabinets, chests of drawers, dressing tables, and the like. Unlike the spacious, salonlike corner where the sofas and beds were located, this section reminded her of a furniture warehouse on the outskirts of the city. The aisles were narrow, and when she passed someone coming from the opposite direction, she had to squeeze by them. Since all the furniture was tall, her field of vision was limited, and since most of the furniture was painted medium or dark brown, it was hard to tell one piece from another. The fresh paint gave off a faint odor, like gasoline, that pervaded the area. It made her lightheaded, like a mild anesthetic. She recalled the time long ago, just before they were married, when she had come with Gōkichi to buy a china cabinet. That time she'd come with the intention of buying something. Now, roaming aimlessly around this place, she had the sensation that the objects lined up in rows were eerily exuding vitality, while her own life was steadily ebbing. Oh, but it wasn't as if she had no objective. Her objective was to locate the woman named Nozawa. Just then, a woman came walking straight toward Yōko. As they were about to have a head-on collision, Yōko was struck by something hard. It was simply that one section of a three-way mirror had opened up, and Yōko, who was walking toward it, had seen her reflection come walking toward her, from out of the mirror. Her eyes were so sunken that her short-bobbed hair looked incongruous. *I'm really exhausted*, she thought when she saw her face. *Why in the world am I in such a sorry state?*

What can be lurking inside a dream? How can a dream, a mere phantasm, manipulate a person during the day like this? Slightly dazed, Yōko mused about these things.

It occurred to her that her impulse to visit the Furniture and Tableware Department hadn't been groundless. Next, she realized that she would have to go to the Toy Department. After all, there had been that six-year-old boy.

AS SHE'D EXPECTED, the confusion that lasted all that day disappeared completely after a night's sleep. But Yōko had become afraid of going to sleep at night. Thinking that if she just slept soundly perhaps she wouldn't dream, she began taking sleeping pills.

Also around this time, she began to mistrust the three years she'd been with Gōkichi, which had seemed so flawless, precisely because of their flawlessness. Beautiful things always conceal an underside that's anything but beautiful, she thought. When she'd first dreamed of Haruyo and Gōkichi, she'd considered the dream preposterous, but now she no longer felt that way. Even Gōkichi carrying on affairs with two or three women, beneath the porcelain-smooth surface of the life he'd led with Yōko, wasn't the least bit preposterous.

If Gōkichi were still alive, she probably could ask him. She probably could even secretly have him investigated. But he was dead. Yōko was painfully aware of having been abandoned without a single means of discovering anything.

AGAIN YŌKO HAD A DREAM about a woman and Gōkichi.

The dream went like this. It began the same way as all the other dreams, with Gōkichi wearing that sullen look on his face. Gōkichi turned around with that expression that was utterly unfamiliar to Yōko. By now Yōko was accustomed to the dream, and in the midst of it she thought, *Oh, here goes this dream again.* For some reason, Gōkichi was riding on a camel. Moreover, he was wearing the kind of long linen or cotton tunic that is worn by desert nomads. It hung in a conical shape, from his neck to midway down the camel's legs. It seemed to be just past dusk in the vast desert; both sand and sky were a dark gray color, tinged with red. That reddish tinge was remarkably deep in just one portion of the sky. The camel began walking, carrying Gōkichi into the distance. The sky steadily darkened, and Yōko's impression that Gōkichi was traveling to the Land of the Dead intensified. Then, in that desert, where it seemed there should be no one besides Gōkichi, Yōko noticed another camel, far ahead of his, advancing into the distance. Riding on that camel was Yōko's classmate from her women's college days, Makimura Mitsue. Mitsue looked around, a smile brimming with joy on her face. It was clear that her smile wasn't directed at Yōko, left behind all alone, but at Gōkichi, who was following Mitsue. *Those two?* thought Yōko, as she stood there, incredulous. The two of them seemed to be traveling to the Land of the Dead at about the same time.

When she woke up, this time Yōko was not at a loss what to do. She knew that going to meet the woman in her dream—as she'd done the previous time and the time before that—was the activity on today's agenda.

Since becoming vulnerable to assaults by her dreams, Yōko felt that she'd strayed far from the realm of mundane life into some murky borderland. She was utterly helpless. If she were subjected to an enemy attack, she could probably fend it off. But since she was being attacked by her dreams, which emerged from some obscure place deep within her, she was totally defenseless.

Anyway, what were these similar dreams that she kept having? They visited her one after another, almost as if someone were taking revenge on her for her three years of happiness. They were stitching a black lining into her cheerful attire.

Yōko got ready and left her home. She was aware that she was moving toward her objective with purposeful precision, like a person who goes out to tend to some important business. The first time, when she'd gone to visit Haruyo, and the next, when she'd gone to meet the department store saleswoman, she'd been nervous, as if she were enacting the continuation of her dream. But now she was composed, like an inveterate criminal working his territory, and she set about her task methodically. She'd visited Haruyo at the beginning of spring, when the fragrance of cherry blossoms was in the air. It had turned into the rainy season without her noticing it. Today, in the intervals between rain, sultry sunlight beat down relentlessly.

To get to Makimura Mitsue's home Yōko had to ride a bus, a national train, and a private train line, then walk a good distance. In the past Yōko had often walked from the station of the private train line to Mitsue's home. One passed through a residential area where, oddly enough, there was only black garden soil in yards that weren't landscaped. After Yōko had married, everything besides her life with Gōkichi had slipped away, and she'd stopped meeting with any of her friends. That lush, fertile-looking black soil that had always caught her attention when she came to this area looked all the more richly black, having absorbed the season's rain.

On the electric poles along the road where she walked, she noticed black-bordered funeral placards that read THE MAKIMURA FAMILY and had arrows pointing toward Mitsue's home. Someone must have died. If Mitsue was in mourning, Yōko couldn't very well talk to her. Bearing this in mind, Yōko turned left at a corner and walked in the direction of the Makimura home.

The hearse was just about to leave. After it passed, five or six cars carrying family members and relatives passed. Yōko looked for Mitsue, but with everyone huddled together in black mourning clothes, it was hard to tell one person from another inside the cars.

"Who passed away?" Yōko asked some people standing by the roadside, feeling embarrassed to be the only person there wearing colorful clothing.

"The oldest daughter," replied a middle-aged woman.

"You mean Mitsue?"

Humid sunlight streamed down from between the clouds. Yōko looked up at the sky. No blue sky was visible, but many long sun rays slanted down, piercing through the white billows of haze.

"It's really sad. She was still so young." The woman began walking away. She was constantly wiping her streaming perspiration.

"I wonder why I wasn't notified about it," mumbled Yōko, as she began walking away with the woman.

People began moving, and their voices began moving with them.

"They say it was uterine cancer."

"She wasn't even married?"

"That I don't know."

"Is uterine cancer fatal?"

"It's because young people don't take care of themselves."

Yōko kept pace with the woman. People's conversations assailed her. The hot moisture in the sunlight collected in the pores on her skin. The women's traditional mourning clothes looked terribly heavy in the heat. Yōko walked along with those black sleeves. She advanced with the scent of blended sweat and powder. Where were these people going? Of course. The funeral was over, so they were returning to the station. Yōko herself was retracing her steps on the road that she'd just taken here.

"Did Mitsue really pass away?" Yōko's own voice sounded as if it were coming from the middle of nowhere.

"She hadn't been well for a long time."

"That's understandable. It's a serious disease."

"Didn't you know about today?" the woman asked. Then the two of them stopped in front of the railroad tracks. A train with about ten cars roared past. Yōko endured the din for a moment before responding.

"Oh, I knew. I received the message last night," she said.

If last night's dream had been an oracle, then perhaps so had the previous dreams. Yōko returned the woman's gaze. She tried to tell if the woman's face registered suspicion toward her for having come to a funeral in colorful clothing, even though she'd been told about it. The woman just kept on wiping perspiration with the palm of her hand. Finally, she took out a handkerchief and patted her face. Brownish foundation came off on the handkerchief.

Yōko drifted away from the people going home from the funeral and found herself walking alone. She rode on the private train line, then on the national line. She felt as if she was lost in thought, yet she wasn't thinking of anything in particular. Suddenly she realized that she'd ridden halfway around a loop line, and she rushed off the train at the next stop. When she saw the station name, she remembered that it was the station where she always got off in order to go to Haruyo's home. That was it. Evidently what she'd been vaguely thinking from a little while before was that she absolutely must meet with Haruyo.

Yōko was buying some Muscat grapes as a house gift at a fruit store in front of the station when someone tapped her on the back. She turned around and saw that it was Haruyo. Apparently Haruyo had just finished her shopping and was about to go home. Her shopping basket was chock full of wrapped packages. Haruyo wasn't her usual self; she had a wanton look in her eyes. The provocative perfume she was wearing intensified that impression.

"I had a strange dream," Yōko blurted out. She immediately realized that she hadn't intended to start a conversation on this note. She felt as if she'd been stimulated by the scent of Haruyo's perfume.

"I have strange dreams, too. These days I'm always having dreams," said Haruyo, as they stood in front of the shop.

"The time I stayed with Gōkichi at the Long Beach Hotel—that's what I dreamed about," said Yōko. She thought it peculiar to begin this sort of conversation in front of the fruit shop, amid the housewives carrying shopping baskets who were going in and out.

"The midsummer ocean must have been beautiful," said Haruyo.

"How did you know?"

"Because we always went there during the summer vacation."

"By 'we' do you mean you and Gōkichi? Do you mean that these days you're always dreaming about those times?"

"What's the matter, Yōko? What on earth is wrong?"

"Well, as you know, I'm the only one who can't swim. You and Gōkichi were swimming side by side, having a race in the pool. Bringing your arms up from the water and over, up and over, the two of you kept swimming, on and on. In a straight line, far out to sea. . . . "

That's right. That was the first dream she'd had about Haruyo and Gōkichi, the one she hadn't been able to remember clearly. No, that wasn't it; at least, that's not all there was to it. Something had happened long ago, when she was in high school. It wasn't a dream. How could she have forgotten such a painful blow? As she was tenderly nursing her wound, casting her eyes downward, looking down even more, then crouching down, from somewhere a great silence had descended, and that milky-white band of silence had covered her wound. Since then, she had completely forgotten the incident: that Mineyama Shōsuke had been stolen from her by her classmate, Tanabe Yuriko. Yōko had been a sophomore in high school. It had happened at the midsummer seashore. Yōko had been walking toward him when Shōsuke, with whom she'd been so close, turned around and gave her an icy look. Then he and Tanabe Yuriko—just the two of them—went swimming far out to sea, while Yōko, who couldn't swim, was left standing on the shore. White light was exploding, reflecting, sparkling everywhere. But darkness stealthily infiltrated that light, and it intensified moment by moment. Yōko went sinking alone through that darkness. When she opened her eyes with a start, as ever, sunlight was glittering everywhere, and it was so dazzling that she shielded her eyes with one hand. As she was wavering drowsily on the border between light and darkness, those two kept swimming farther and farther into the distance, until they were completely out of sight. Then their ardent sighs merged and formed a white column of clouds that rose, glimmering, over the horizon.

THE BUZZER SOUNDED. Yōko got up from the sofa, feeling resolute. Men's voices were audible in the hallway outside the door.

"Thank you for your trouble," said Yōko as she opened the door.

"We went to the wrong apartment complex. We thought it was Number 405 in that building across the way. We went up to the fourth floor and came down, and here we had to come up to the fourth floor again."

As the man wearing the suit spoke, the other man, in work clothes, struggled to lift the cardboard carton at his feet. It was about 50 centimeters in length, width, and height.

"Surely it's not so heavy," said Yōko, picturing that slender, fragile body in the bathing suit.

The two men propped open the door, and then together they carried the carton into the apartment. Yōko followed them, walking calmly into the dining area.

"Where do you want us to put it?" asked the man in the suit. The man in the work clothes still said nothing.

"On the table," Yōko replied. This was the place that she had decided upon.

"Y'oughta put 'er on the veranda, dontcha think?" The man in work clothes finally opened his mouth. He had a terrible rustic accent.

"I'm the one who bought it. Please do as I say." Yōko said this in a firm tone of voice, so the two men stared at her in unison.

When the carton had been placed on the table, Yōko held out her personal stamp.

"It'll look nice here, but I still think y'oughta give 'er a little sunshine." The man in work clothes looked ruefully back toward the veranda, where white, early summer sunlight was streaming.

Yōko did not respond.

She stamped the sale slip; then the men left. A smell lingered in the room. She couldn't tell whether it was the men's body odor or cigarette smoke or the dirt on their clothes. She quickly opened all the windows to air the place out.

She approached the table and put her ear close to the cardboard carton. Maybe it was frightened; there wasn't a sound. Yōko made a clucking noise with the tip of her tongue, and she tapped the carton with her fingertips. Inside something moved sluggishly, then there was silence again.

Yōko had mulled over various possibilities. Since the girl's name was Yuriko, which means "lily," she had first thought of using some large, soft white bird. But upon further consideration, she hit upon the idea of using a bird that would besmirch that name, an ugly crow, for instance. But there was no store that sold crows. Besides, throttling a white, soft neck with her hands was more likely to yield a realistic sensation. She had never touched a crow, but she imagined that if she tried twisting the neck of such a coarse bird she would probably only scrape her own hands. After much deliberation, she settled on a parrot. She decided that the more splendid the creature, the better. Having a splendid creature as adversary, rather than a delicate one or an ugly one, would make her deed all the crueler. Anyway, the vital thing was to bring her plan to fruition. Splendor and cruelty would make a perfect pair.

She had made the rounds of many shops. When she discovered the crimson parrot, her heart throbbed with a dark pleasure.

Inside the box on this table, right now the crimson parrot was leading a quiet, cozy existence. Yōko wouldn't think of opening the box to peer at it. She wanted to leave it in the darkness as much as possible. She wanted it to make it feel suffocated in the darkness. Should she leave it like that for days? Should she deprive it of food and let it feed on the darkness in the box until little by little it went mad? No, Yōko resolved to carry out her scheme that night, as planned.

Without even looking, she could picture the parrot in its cage in the box very vividly. Its crimson plumage was a garish hue. It was a wonder that such a shade existed in nature. The color was rich and opaque, just as if someone had dyed the bird with a syrupy red ink. The parrot had its gaudy wings neatly tucked away, as if it were concealing a secret, but it was stretching its clear eyes wide open.

Soon I won't be having those dreams anymore. Mother has taught me an excellent remedy, thought Yōko, as she stood listening raptly to the gentle rustling inside the box.

Foxfire

Ichiko ought to have been used to the crowds that she encountered while commuting to and from her job. But these days, she
no longer was. Was it her own fault that she was no longer used
to something that she'd once been used to? Had she actually not
been used to it in the first place? It made no difference what kind
of crowd it was. Whether she was walking among the droves of
businessmen in the morning or evening or the droves of various
kinds of people streaming through the city during the day, she
would sometimes suddenly come to a standstill. At those times, a
certain dread would arise in her, like the tip of a needle. What if
someone amid this dark swarm were to cry out in a shrill voice,
"It's her!" and point a finger at Ichiko? Then every person in the
crowd would turn toward her in unison. Incited by the person
who'd shouted, the nameless, faceless mob would begin heading

toward her. The horde of people would rush straight at Ichiko and run her down.

Lately she'd begun having that fantasy. So she made a point of not standing still while in a crowd. She told herself that she should just imitate the people walking all around her and walk as if she'd lost her name and her face. She should try not to make a face that was at all conspicuous. Apparently it was unacceptable to reveal any individuality on one's face. She should walk with bated breath, so as not to be noticed, not to be noticed by that dreadful someone who would point at her and shout, "It's her!" She should wear the same protective coloring as everyone else in the crowd, and assume the expression of a dullard as she walked. But she wouldn't know where her accuser was. That person wasn't the least bit distinctive. Any one of the people in the crowd could suddenly become that person.

"Someone was looking for you, Miss Nozawa. Right here."

Ichiko snapped out of her reverie when she heard the voice. The crowd streamed through this department store, too, just as in her imaginary city. She'd now worked here for four years, but compared to when she began working here, the inside of the department store, especially on Sundays, had turned into a mob scene. But here Ichiko was somewhat protected, because she was confined behind the accessories counter. Objects of fake beauty, in various shapes and hues, were crammed together in the glass case that separated her from the people passing by.

The voice that had called to her belonged to Yoshie, who worked at the necktie counter where Ichiko herself had worked until a week ago.

"Someone came to see you," said Yoshie, who happened to pass by.

"Me?"

I wonder who, Ichiko thought. At that moment it seemed to her that there wasn't a single person in the world who would come to see her. Actually, that wasn't necessarily true, but perhaps the reason she instantly felt that way was because she'd just been imagining the sensation of walking all alone in a crowd.

"Someone who doesn't know your name," said Yoshie, and began to walk away.

"You say someone who doesn't know my name came to see me?" Ichiko leaned slightly forward over the glass case.

"But the person described your facial features exactly. It was almost uncanny. She said, 'a woman with thick eyebrows, whose right eye seems to become slightly larger than her left eye.' It's true, isn't it. I realized it after the person had pointed it out."

Ichiko glared at Yoshie over the glass case.

"There. That's just the look the person was talking about, I suppose." Yoshie smiled, flashing her white dentures, then walked off.

Uneasiness welled up in Ichiko, and she rushed out into the aisle.

"Who was it?" She grabbed the shoulder of Yoshie's uniform as she was returning to her sales counter.

"I have no idea. Someone I've never seen. Of course, I didn't get a name."

"It doesn't make sense."

"The person seemed rather persistent."

"What did they come to ask?"

"Nothing. And yet, the person was persistent."

Ichiko's uneasiness began congealing, like gelatin, into bafflement.

"When was this?"

"Just now. Look—over there."

Ichiko looked toward the necktie counter that Yoshie was pointing at. Far beyond it she could see the front entrance of the store, and through the glass door there she could see the crowds streaming by. Although it was spring, a cold wind was blowing today. Pedestrians were walking alone, separately, huddled up as if to shield themselves from that cold air. They had to walk as if they were nameless and faceless, or else they would be violating the rules of the sidewalk in the city. Again, in her imagination, Ichiko had the sensation that she was moving along with a crowd. She had to walk with the same bestial dullness, with the same blind sturdiness as other people. No matter how stylishly she dressed, her style had to match other people's, and she had to walk in the same rhythm as other people. She shouldn't have an intense gaze that made her right eye appear larger than her left eye. Someone who astutely noticed that might follow Ichiko, like that person had, all the way to a sales counter in a department store, pointing at her and saying, "It's her!" Yes, it was only natural that the person didn't know Ichiko's name.

"Miss Nozawa, you seem exhausted these days," said Yoshie.

Even after returning to the accessories counter, Ichiko felt engulfed in fatigue. Since she'd turned twenty-eight, there were times when every single cell in her head felt heavy. It was as if the cells were encrusted with sticky soot, and no matter how much she slept, she couldn't free herself from that sensation.

A middle-aged female customer asked to see a thick gold chain inside the glass case, so Ichiko took it out. Then the customer asked to see a pendant that had an imitation turquoise stone hanging on a thin silver chain. Next, the customer asked for a necklace consisting of many intertwined strands of beads of various colors. After those three items were on top of the glass case, the customer continued to run her gaze back and forth over other objects in the case. She was evidently trying to choose an item that cost around 3,000 *yen*. She was accompanied by a girl who appeared to be in third or fourth grade, and the girl, too, was running her eyes over various items, just like the woman. Judging from the girl's clothing, her mother was rather negligent. When the girl glanced up at Ichiko, the whites of her eyes looked yellowish. The customer took a long time to decide. In these four years, Ichiko had acquired the ability to wait on customers like this without becoming irritated or brusque. The customer requested yet another pendant. It was one with a big cloisonné ornament hanging on it. Just as it seemed that she would buy that one, she again picked up the bead necklace and stared at it. Her face appeared as if she were lost in contemplation. For some reason, Ichiko was intrigued by that expression.

Then, beneath her gaze Ichiko sensed an ominous, faint air vibration. Her eyes were still fastened on the customer, but she noticed on the lower edge of her field of vision that the imitation turquoise pendant, which was on top of the glass case, was slipping away at imperceptible speed. The movement was clearly visible because of the brilliant color of the blue stone. The very long brown muffler that was wound around the girl's neck hung down on the glass case, forming a mound there; the pendant was being pulled beneath that mound. The girl had her face turned toward her mother, who was examining the other necklace, and both elbows resting on the glass. Her right hand was hidden in the mound of the muffler, and her left hand was casually moving back and forth on the glass. Evidently she was moving her left hand that way in order to deflect attention from the movement of the pendant.

Since Ichiko had started working at the department store, it was the first time that this sort of thing had happened at her counter. She decided to pretend not to notice anything until the pendant had been completely engulfed beneath the girl's muffler. She felt like she was being a bit mean. Because if she protested, the mischief would be thwarted in midstream, and the girl would be able to say that she hadn't done anything wrong. Ichiko felt that she had to let her go through with the deed.

When the turquoise stone had disappeared beneath the muffler, Ichiko finally turned and stared straight at the girl. The girl looked directly back at Ichiko, too. Both of them seemed to be calculating the passage of time, as if they were performing a countdown. The girl's eyes were large. But Ichiko couldn't rid herself of the impression that the whites of her eyes were slightly turbid. Her fine, slightly yellowish hair was parted down the middle and secured by pins on the right and left sides, but the pins looked like they were about to slide down. Because of that, her hair was disheveled. Tendrils of fine hair glistened around her perspiring brow, and her whole face was pale. Perhaps because she felt cornered by Ichiko's stare, she began to seem to be panting. But on close observation, she was deathly silent. Her mouth was motionless and there was no sound of breathing. Somewhere inside her she was panting, but on the surface she was remarkably still. Her large eyes gradually widened. Raw emotion was becoming more visible on her face moment by moment; Ichiko couldn't tell whether that was terror or hatred or joy. But the girl remained utterly silent.

The interaction between Ichiko and the child had nearly ceased. But the muffler hanging down on the glass case was jiggling slightly up and down, as if there were a warm living creature concealed in it. Something whizzed beneath it, then instantly the muffler became just a muffler and flattened out. Ichiko couldn't tell where the object that the girl had held in her right hand had ended up. The top of the glass case was on a level with the girl's chest, so Ichiko couldn't see whether she had pockets down below.

Just then it dawned on Ichiko that there was no relationship whatsoever between the middle-aged woman customer, who was still lost in thought, and the girl. When she realized this, the brazenness of the girl, who for several minutes had convincingly played the role of a child accompanying her mother, wafted like a bittersweet fragrance from that slender body toward Ichiko.

The girl suddenly left the accessories counter. She no doubt had a child's typical insouciance, for she immediately looked relieved to be free. Ichiko pushed the buzzer that was at the counter. It was an emergency device for contacting the security office. She kept an eye on the girl's receding figure while she waited for the security guard to come running. But the guard didn't appear.

"I'll go see," Ichiko murmured.

She left the message for the security guard with her co-worker at the same sales counter, then walked off. Sales clerks weren't supposed to deal with such incidents themselves, but a curiosity that bordered on cruelty had taken hold of Ichiko. She probably would-n't be reprimanded just for observing.

Ichiko thought that she'd lost sight of the child when suddenly she appeared in a gap in the stream of customers. As Ichiko had expected, the girl apparently didn't intend to leave the store. When a person succeeds at shoplifting, they usually want to try it once or twice again. The girl traipsed down the aisle as if she were intoxicated. She passed one sales counter after another, each separated from the next by a large pillar. She wore a short coat like a raincoat, and that woolen muffler dangled down her back. The pleats of her skirt jiggled back and forth, and beneath them stretched those overly slender legs. Ichiko couldn't tell whether they were bare or covered with cream-colored stockings, but her legs looked terribly white.

At the far end of the store, the girl came to a halt in front of the counter selling western-style wigs. She must have come here any number of times and planned her strategy, because she immediately went up to the counter and snatched a chestnut-colored wig in a pageboy style. There was a crowd of women picking up wigs, putting them down, and trying them on in front of mirrors. The girl stood in front of a mirror and all too deftly popped the wig onto her head. Ichiko was watching from behind a pillar far away. She felt as if the thumping of her heart must be audible to those around her. It was the girl's breast that should have been pounding, but instead it was Ichiko's; her entire body was throbbing. She was observing the scene from the side, so she couldn't see the expression on the girl's face. What she could see very clearly was that the girl was scrutinizing herself from various angles. And yet, she could easily blend in with all the other women who were doing the same thing.

What did the child intend to do? The trick that she'd used to procure the pendant—hiding it under her long muffler and pulling it toward her—could hardly be adapted to her present situation.

Suddenly the girl slipped away from the spot as casually as she had approached it. She walked off, just like that. She glided along, her gait exuding her high spirits. Not a single person had noticed.

Ichiko was astonished. Not only by the scheme of stealing a wig simply by leaving it on one's head, but because the girl seemed to have metamorphosed into a different person. Until moments before she'd looked like someone who smelled from not having bathed in days, but that impression had mysteriously vanished. Ichiko could now see that her white legs were bare, after all. The pale color of her legs and the glossy chestnut wig on her head created an elegant contrast. The combination seemed to have transformed the girl into a westerner.

The child suddenly whirled around, noticed Ichiko, and stopped in her tracks. Their gazes met. But the creature who shortly before had been a mere sniveling ragamuffin now stood there with the haughty air of a fairy princess. Finally the security guard caught up with them and stood beside Ichiko. People were constantly passing between Ichiko and the girl. The two continued to stare unflinchingly at each other. The child's panting, still invisible from the outside, seemed to be growing more agitated by the moment. She was looking more and more like a small animal, trapped at the end of a blind alley, that was stretching its eyes wide open as it awaited a fatal blow. She radiated a sensuous aura; whether its source was terror or hatred or joy was impossible to say.

The girl suddenly began walking. The security guard went after her. Ichiko followed them slowly. The receding figure in the chestnut wig moved agilely ahead, cutting through the crowds in the department store. Ichiko saw the guard catch up to the girl just before she reached the exit and begin to talk to her. Then Ichiko discreetly followed the pair as they headed toward the security guard's office. No one had noticed anything. It was as if an invisible rainbow had formed over this place where so many eyes were glancing around and where so many bodies were jostling against each other. And along that invisible arc, a crime and a chase and an arrest were in progress.

As soon as Ichiko entered the security office, she was startled by the sort of cry that one hears at a zoo. It was a cry that blended something low and rumbling with something shrill that zigzagged up through the air. The girl, still wearing the western-style wig, was writhing on the sofa and crying.

"My stomach hurts! My stomach hurts!" she was wailing in the intervals between sobs.

The security guard signaled to Ichiko. Apparently he felt that under the circumstances, a woman ought to deal with the girl. Ichiko approached and tried to touch her. The girl flailed her legs as uncouthly as if she were a boy. Ichiko caught a glimpse of two or three layers of lace-trimmed pink panties. Maybe she stole them, went into the bathroom, and put them on. The garments weren't appropriate for a girl of her age.

"Shall I call a doctor?" Ichiko asked the security guard, who was sitting on a chair, holding some documents.

"What for?" replied the guard curtly.

"Maybe she's really in pain." Ichiko rose and looked down at the girl. She urgently wanted to clarify something. She couldn't verbalize what it was. She felt that she was being spirited away, along with the girl, on that invisible rainbow.

Ichiko stayed with the sobbing child while the security guard went to call the doctor on the premises. The earnestness in the girl's sobbing kept it from seeming feigned, but if one listened closely, there also seemed to be a slightly hollow ring to it.

Ichiko recalled an incident from the previous summer.

She'd been lounging around her apartment with nothing to do, steeped in the stifling humidity of early evening, when she heard the piercing sound of glass shattering. She went into the dark room next door and could dimly make out a large star-shaped hole in the window. She stood there in a daze, wondering why the window was broken, since she hadn't broken it. At that time of the day when the humidity rises rapidly, there's tension in the air, as if a demon were afoot. When Ichiko finally turned on the light, she saw a rock about the size of an egg lying on the tatami-covered floor, mixed in with the glass fragments. It finally occurred to her that someone had broken the window, and then she looked outside. There was a narrow road, and since the streetlights were off, it was nearly dark. A portion of that darkness was furtively retreating, step by step, along the cinder block wall across the road. Apparently it was a boy. A boy had thrown the rock. As soon as she realized that, Ichiko dashed out of her room. She stood in the front entrance of her apartment and stared in the direction the boy had fled. There was no car traffic, and in contrast to the large thoroughfares where one is overwhelmed by auto exhaust and thunderous noise, the street was utterly silent. Ichiko guessed that the boy must have turned left at the next street corner. She ran briskly. Mortar or cinder block walls ran all along the road, so there was no foliage in which to hide. Sure enough, shortly past the corner where he had turned, the boy was pressed up against the wall like a lizard. He stared straight back at Ichiko. His expression wasn't clear. Ichiko approached him quickly. The boy began to run. There was no contest; at least Ichiko thought so. But it was only after chasing him for a hundred meters that she managed to nab him. No else one was around. The boy's arm that Ichiko had grabbed was terribly slimy and warm. A repulsive sensation, as if she'd actually clutched a lizard, coursed through her body from her palm. Then suddenly the boy began to scream. She thought that he'd begun to cry, but no, he was actually screaming. He was wearing a sleeveless undershirt, and he was nearly naked. Greasy sweat oozed from his entire body. That clamminess, that queer scream—Ichiko instinctively released her grip. But she couldn't let the boy escape, so she grabbed the belt on his pants.

"Why did you throw the rock?" she asked, with a feeling of dread. "Breaking a window and running away, then what?" she pressed, not hoping to receive an answer but to get to the bottom of this vague sense of dread.

"Did you do it because you knew it was wrong? That I can understand. But that wasn't it, was it? Why, then? Why?" Ichiko kept after him.

The boy continued to scream. Ichiko heard the sound of windows and doors that faced the street being opened. She realized that people were sticking their heads out and watching them. She was forced to release her grip. The boy fled, his existence becoming ever more fragile, like a thread of caramel. The screaming subsided. Ichiko sensed that somewhere, far out in space, a face was sticking out its tongue at her. The echo of that berserk scream resounded in her ears for a long time.

When the guard entered the security office with the doctor, the girl was still sobbing. Even if she was putting on an act, to continue crying in a loud voice for ten minutes must be quite a feat, Ichiko thought. If that kind of power lurks in a child, it must be a power that surpasses an adult's comprehension.

"The doctor is here, so let's have him examine you," Ichiko said, and she moved toward the girl. She had never liked children, and besides, she was perplexed by that inhuman kind of crying.

"Miss Nozawa, don't be so nice to her. I have to conduct an investigation now," said the guard, drawing near.

The girl abruptly stopped sobbing. She glanced at the guard out of one eye, as if peering through a gap in the noise she was making. Then again her wailing reverberated through the room. The chestnut-colored hair of the wig gently bobbed, and the lacy pink panties flashed intermittently. The imitation turquoise pendant must have been in her pocket.

The doctor approached, so Ichiko and the security guard both withdrew a bit.

"What's your name?" said the doctor.

Again the wailing paused, and the girl gave a quick glance up. But this glance seemed slightly different from her previous one. Ichiko couldn't say what was different about it, but she watched as the girl completely stopped crying and slowly raised her chestnut-colored head.

"I'm Ruriko," said the girl to the doctor, undulating her slender body.

"Say your last name clearly," said the doctor, as he knelt down beside the sofa where the girl was lying.

"Yoshimura Ruriko."

Aha. There was a snortlike laugh. The security guard was turning the pages of the documents spread out on the table. A list of chronic offenders was sent to him from various other department stores. In response to Ichiko's inquiring glance, the guard returned a glance that said, "No."

"I hear your stomach hurts. Where does it hurt?" The doctor began to place his hand on the girl's stomach.

"Oooh, don't *do* that." The girl's voice rose coyly.

Ichiko scrutinized the doctor's face, feeling as if the girl had awakened her to something. She had become aware, for the first time, of the "male" within this middle-aged doctor whom she'd seen any number of times.

"Weren't you crying? Were you just pretending?"

The girl didn't reply, but reacted disdainfully to the word 'pretending.'

"If you tell us your name and address, then hand over everything you stole, we'll let you go home." The guard sat down on a chair and spoke in a businesslike way.

"I haven't stolen a thing," the girl retorted.

The doctor stood up and took two or three steps back. Using both hands, the girl began tidying her disheveled hair and rumpled clothing, so the previous scene seemed to take on a lewd significance. The girl carried on like that for a long time. She seemed well aware that by doing so she could maintain the men's attention.

The doctor withdrew and began to head for the door. The girl's crying began again.

"You say your stomach hurts, but I can't know where it hurts unless I examine you." The doctor knelt in front of the sofa again.

"Isn't that enough?" said Ichiko. If the doctor was oblivious, that irritated her, but if he was fully aware, that irritated her too.

"What did you take, Ruriko?" said the doctor.

"That wig and—I'm sure it's in her pocket—a pendant. Those two things."

Ichiko spoke on the girl's behalf. She couldn't bring herself to mention the panties. But that particular mischief floated clearly before her mind's eye. After snatching those at the lingerie counter, she went into the ladies room and pulled them on over the pair she was wearing. The girl's deed was transmitted vividly to Ichiko, right down to the sensation of warmth.

"A wig? A pendant?" The girl eyed Ichiko with a foxy look on her face.

The security guard was filling out the forms spread in front of him on the table.

"Tell me your name and address." He was tapping the paper with the base of his fountain pen, as if to hurry her reply.

"Yoshimura Ruriko, ooooo Itabashi-ku, Tokyo," the girl said in a dry voice. She sounded like a different person from when she'd spoken to the doctor.

"Your school?"

No answer.

"If you answer the questions and say you're sorry, you'll be able to leave."

"Sorry? Say I'm sorry?"

"Come on now, hand over the wig and the pendant. Take everything out of your pockets and put it on top of the table."

The girl sprang to her feet. She stood on tiptoe, spread both arms out horizontally, twirled around once, like a ballerina, and in the end beamed, at no one in particular.

"The wig belongs to me. I bought it," said the girl, placing her hand on her head for emphasis. "When you say 'pendant,' do you mean this? I bought this, too." She drew the object out of her coat pocket and showed it. Nine 10-*yen* coins came out along with it.

"Don't play games with us!" It was the doctor who shouted.

Again the girl became coquettish. She fell silent, turned kitten-ish, and her entire body became pliant. She aligned her arms pre-cisely, pressed them together, swung them to the right, and then swung them to the left. She made various balletlike gestures, press-ing her hands together, laying them against her right cheek, then against her left cheek. The pendant was clasped in her hands, and with each movement the girl made, the blue stone twirled around. Ichiko noticed that the label on the pendant had been removed.

"Miss Nozawa, take the wig off her," said the guard.

As Ichiko removed it from the girl's head, she felt as if she were peeling off her scalp. A bestial odor rose from the girl's hair and mingled with Ichiko's sense of cruelty. Sure enough, the price label had been removed at some point from the wig, too.

"You see? You see?" crowed the girl brazenly, as if she'd exposed Ichiko's ulterior motive.

The department store's trademark was clearly on the two items, but proof that they were stolen goods had been deftly removed.

The girl began crying again. She seemed about to collapse, so the doctor put his arm around her. But the magic had evaporated; she was reduced to the former bedraggled little girl. She became childlike as a sparrow and just kept sobbing against the doctor's chest. The doctor, too, without realizing it, had lost his masculine allure and had turned into an ordinary father figure.

The security guard looked at Ichiko as if to say, "What shall we do?" Ichiko was standing there in a daze. There was no proof any-where that the girl had taken either the wig or the pendant. The whole incident seemed to be her own crazy dream.

"Maybe you ought to take her home. She seems kind of abnor-mal. This probably isn't enough money for her to get home, either," said the guard to Ichiko, pointing at the nine 10-*yen* coins.

Ichiko changed into her street clothes and began to walk. The girl sluggishly followed her. It would take forty or fifty minutes by sub-way to reach the address that the girl had given a little while before.

They walked along, surrounded by the crowds returning home from their jobs. If Ichiko were to stand still so as not to be swept along by that swarm, if she were to ponder something during that brief pause—no, the crowd would absolutely not permit such things. The crowd would notice immediately, point their fingers, and shout, "It's her!" then stampede her. Those people, who until then had each been separate, would probably converge and rush toward the single point that Ichiko represented, as if they were obeying a law of physics. Because Ichiko was inert; she was a cipher; she was a void. But it wasn't only that. It was because she'd momentarily indulged in the superfluous act of pondering something.

But today, for a change, was different for Ichiko. Because she was with the girl. She was walking with the girl on the extension of what seemed like an invisible rainbow. But her feelings toward the girl included something akin to the dread that a slug or a lizard inspires.

"You must be in elementary school." The child couldn't possibly be in junior high school, Ichiko thought. "How old are you? Around nine, I suppose. Probably nine, aren't you."

What sort of family was the girl from? If you were to separate a child from its family—the ordinary sort of family that you find everywhere—would it turn out to be like this child? Would a demon, invisible when the child was with its family, emerge when the child was alone?

"Did you come all the way to a distant department store just to do that?"

Really, there was no way of knowing what a child was plotting. If you could look inside its head with a special kind of microscope, maybe you would see a slug or a lizard.

"Yoshimura Ruriko—that's a nice name." Ichiko went on chatting to herself.

After getting off at the subway station, they had to walk for over ten minutes. The girl took the lead and went into a huge apartment complex. This was the place whose address was ooooo Itabashi-ku,

Tokyo. All sorts of buildings—square, star-shaped, single family homes, rectangular townhouses—went on and on, one after another. The girl entered a building marked Building H, Section B. When they were on the third floor, in front of apartment #312, she spoke for the first time, to say, "Here." Sure enough, there was a nameplate that read "Yoshimura." The iron door was coated with white dust, and the box for milk had come off and was lying on the floor of the hall.

The girl yanked open the unlocked door and went inside.

ON HER DAYS OFF, Ichiko was in the habit of lounging around her apartment, listening to music. On her way to and from work she encountered crowds, and while at work, too, she encountered crowds; this was her daily routine. So on her days off, she wanted to encounter something abstract.

But today, stray thoughts intruded on the music.

"Miss Nozawa, come here a minute. You remember that someone came to see you the other day? That person came again." Yoshie, from the necktie counter, had come over the day before yesterday to tell her that.

"It's like blackmail," replied Ichiko reflexively.

"My, what a strange thing to say." Yoshie's face was cheerful.

"The person doesn't know my name, right?"

"So it can't be blackmail."

"Someone whose right eye becomes bigger than her left eye when she looks at you—that was a reference to me, obviously. How awful; it's as if my defects were being pointed out to me."

"No, no, that's not so. Don't get worked up over nothing."

The two of them walked toward the necktie counter as they conversed. When Ichiko looked in the direction where Yoshie was pointing, she saw a young woman leaning over the glass case and peering in.

"A woman?" asked Ichiko, a bit surprised.

"What sort of person did you think it was?" When Yoshie said that, Ichiko realized that even though she'd been so anxious, she had neglected to consider such details as sex and age about her visitor. Anyway, she faced the woman and walked straight toward her.

"I'm Nozawa Ichiko," she said, standing by the woman's side.

The woman who looked up appeared far younger than she had at a distance. She looked like she might be a student.

"Oh, no!" cried Yoshie, and Ichiko saw her clap her hand to her mouth, which was open in alarm.

Afterward Yoshie told her that it wasn't the woman who had come looking for her the other day. But at least Ichiko now knew that the person was a young woman. Still, like a fish that slips through one's fingers, the young woman's identity eluded her. Since she hadn't the slightest idea who she might be, Ichiko was left mystified.

"I wonder why someone who doesn't know me would come to see me," Ichiko said when they were on their lunch break.

"She must have mistaken you for someone else," said Yoshie, somewhat sick of the subject.

"What can it mean that someone whom I don't know, who doesn't even know my name, comes to see me?"

"You act as if you have a guilty conscience."

"Guilty, guilty. . . . Now that you mention it, I seem to feel guilty for being alive."

"You think too deeply. You're exhausted."

Yoshie had simply reached the same conclusion again.

Ichiko turned off the radio, which was playing modern jazz, and went out, carrying a shopping bag. It was morning, so there weren't many people in the supermarket, and the place felt spacious. The building was relatively new, and the floor, ceiling, walls, and shelves were smooth and shiny. The food products wrapped in plastic were smooth and shiny too.

It's like being in a foreign country, Ichiko thought, although she'd never been to a foreign country. She must have felt that way because it was a different time of day from when she stopped here on her way home from work.

As she was shopping for food, something that sounded like a bird's cry reverberated throughout the supermarket. Of course, it was a child's voice. But Ichiko's instinct wouldn't yield to her reason; she couldn't bring herself to decide which of the two it was. So without choosing between them, she continued to shop, listening to that voice. Rather, it would be more accurate to say that she was forced to listen to it. It would be impossible to tune out a voice that loud. The child wasn't within Ichiko's range of sight. Its voice seemed to be in collusion with that girl's sobbing, and with the screaming of the boy who broke the window. Each one was different, but they definitely had something inexpressible in common.

Ichiko tossed dried mushrooms, lemons, and green onions into her basket. The poor vegetables were suffocated by the plastic. Price labels had been stuck on each one; they'd been reduced to objects that were powerless except as commodities.

It's like being in a foreign country, Ichiko again thought.

The child's voice sounded closer. When she glanced in its direction, an uncouth-looking man wearing sunglasses appeared, holding a child by the hand. Ichiko couldn't tell if the child was a girl or a boy, but it was wearing red-striped, bell-bottom trousers. It was too young to walk yet, but the man seemed to be pulling it by the hand, and the child was doing a crawl-like walk on the dirty floor. The man, who was apparently the father, was dragging it along like a sack of potatoes.

"I botcha bert, I botcha bert," the man was saying. Apparently he was trying to pacify the child who was emitting that birdlike shriek.

Ichiko's hearing felt deranged. She couldn't understand those words for the life of her.

The man and child walked around and around like that in the nearly empty supermarket.

"I botcha bert, I botcha bert," the man said again.

Ichiko's sensation of being in a foreign country intensified. As if to complete the picture, a woman appeared. Her vulgar looks surpassed those of Sophia Loren, thanks to her makeup. Then the family trio left the store together. The woman was evidently pregnant.

She must have a monster inside her, thought Ichiko, as she watched them disappear.

Only after she'd finished her shopping did it dawn on her that those incomprehensible words had been "I bought sherbet."

Perhaps because of the strange mood that the experience had induced in her, Ichiko suddenly felt like going to that huge apartment complex, even though she was carrying a shopping bag and the trip took more than thirty minutes. It was a weekday morning, so the girl was probably in school. Maybe Ichiko's curiosity to see what sort of parents the girl had had been stimulated by witnessing the parents of that child in the supermarket.

The huge apartment complex was a white maze. It was white, but people's grime had seeped into the whiteness. Everything was crumbling, so slowly that the process was imperceptible. Laundry was fluttering madly in the wind. It was a pale yellowish wind. The white underwear of the residents was probably yellowing, having been dried many times. Even so, the housewives would probably go on vigorously washing it over and over, in an attempt to reverse that process. Between the rows of concrete buildings were paths where the wind whipped around, and as Ichiko walked along, she was buffeted by it from all directions. Her hair fluttered, and it seemed to squeak as it mixed with the dust. The children in the complex scampered around in the gusty wind.

On the third floor of Section B, Building H, Ichiko knocked at the door of apartment #312. An old woman came to the door.

"What is it?" she asked.

"I was just in the neighborhood, so I stopped by. How is Yoshimura Ruriko doing? I'm the one who brought her home the other day from the city when she wasn't feeling well," said Ichiko, trying to peer inside the home.

"Yoshimura Ruriko?" repeated the old woman in a puzzled tone. She was probably about seventy years old, but her looks weren't ravaged by the years, and there was something buoyant about her.

"Yes. Is she your grandchild?"

"I'm single."

"Oh, my. Doesn't Yoshimura Ruriko live here?"

"I've never heard of a child named Ruriko."

But she opened this door and went inside, Ichiko thought. She was on the verge of asking the old woman if she'd been robbed recently, but she restrained herself. Because she felt as if that girl, so radiant after donning the chestnut-colored wig, had passed through this doorway and vanished like magic.

"So there was no such child?" murmured Ichiko, as if talking to herself.

THE EXPRESS TRAIN of the Chūō line was carrying Ichiko from her hometown to Tokyo. Light streamed in through the wide windows. The car was pleasantly warm, and warmth permeated her body, too. Outside the window green groves of trees glistened, and the sky overflowed with light. The three days that Ichiko had spent in her hometown, on vacation from her job, had been bathed in that light. It was becoming ever more replete with the passage of spring, and Ichiko felt rejuvenated. From before she'd gone on vacation, that process had already become noticeable.

"You seem greatly recovered," said Yoshie.

Recovered from what? Ichiko had wanted to ask, but she remained silent. It wasn't as if she was mentally ill.

"You know, for instance, when your stomach hurts and you're groaning in pain. At the time you think, this hurts so badly I'll never recover. You're wrong, though; you always recover. But there are things that you absolutely never recover from. One is the temperament you're born with," Ichiko had responded.

Now that it was spring, here and there you could see heat hazes. Ichiko had often encountered them in her hometown. A rippling, transparent flame would be flaring up from tile roofs and riverbanks and stone walls, just as if someone had struck a match and ignited them. For some reason, heat hazes made Ichiko think of foxfire. She pictured a reddish yet transparent flame spurting up from the gaping mouth of a fox. She didn't actually know what foxfire was. And yet she was haunted by the feeling that she knew very well what foxfire was. She had the irritating sensation that she was on the verge of remembering, but couldn't quite recall when and where she had come to know it.

At K Station two boys who were apparently brothers got on the train, accompanied by a woman of around thirty-four or thirty-five. The woman wasn't fashionably dressed, and her face was intelligent and unadorned. The good breeding typical of children of a fine family was evident in her sons' appearance. They weren't wearing especially stylish clothes, which, conversely, suggested their mother's confidence in them. The older one was eleven or twelve, the younger probably eight or nine. Ichiko was sitting in a compartment on the left side of the aisle, and the two boys were in one on the right, two compartments ahead of Ichiko. They were sitting side by side, their backs to her. The younger boy was sitting in the seat by the aisle. Their mother was sitting on the left, like Ichiko, so Ichiko couldn't see her. Ichiko was staring absentmindedly, without actually looking closely, at the back of the younger boy, whom she could see very well.

By and by, that boy leaned his upper body up against the armrest. Then he kept moving in that direction until he had rotated his upper body halfway around, so that Ichiko could see his face. Then he turned toward her even more. Ichiko's gaze and the boy's gaze met. He had black, round, adorable eyes. She could clearly see their upturned eyelashes. From the time the two boys had entered the car with their mother, Ichiko had felt the atmosphere around her mysteriously brighten. Now she realized that that radiance originated in the younger boy's face. The older brother's features were perfectly symmetrical and a bit severe, but there was something slightly lopsided about the younger one's. The boy's tender age combined with that imbalance to charming effect.

After the eyes of the boy and Ichiko had met, immediately the boy began returning to his original position, little by little. He reversed the series of actions he had just performed, until he faced forward. Then the line of his left shoulder relaxed a bit and the flesh there seemed to soften. As if enticed by Ichiko's steady gaze, he began moving toward her; then he slowly turned around, and again his head spun around to face her. The boy's eyes came to rest precisely on Ichiko's, this time not by coincidence. Those eyes seemed to be returning to hers to confirm something that they'd overlooked before. Then Ichiko smiled. As if startled by that, the boy quickly resumed his original position. But again his head whirled around, and his eyes pounced on Ichiko. Each time, the expression in the boy's eyes changed a bit. They gradually began to resemble the eyes of a man looking at a woman. Ichiko calculated the difference in age between herself and the boy. At the same time, she was reminded of that girl's flirtatious behavior toward the doctor in the security guard's office several weeks before.

Ichiko's suspiciousness about the girl's address had continued to nag at her, so she'd gone again to visit the old woman whose name was Yoshimura. Various concrete shapes were crammed together in that apartment complex—rectangles, stars, crescents. If the address "Section B, Building H, Room #312" hadn't been firmly engraved in her mind, Ichiko felt as though she would wander around and around the maze of similar buildings that repeated themselves over and over. The sky was blue and completely dry. The perfect weather for doing laundry continued. On every veranda of the huge complex laundry fluttered in the breeze, like banners hailing the robust life force of the housewives who lived there.

The broad paved paths ran vertically and horizontally, ran diagonally, ran in semicircles. Ichiko walked on paths that sloped from left to right. Why were they sloping this much? Had they been paved without the ground first being leveled? The people who walked on these every day must feel terribly unbalanced, Ichiko thought. She suddenly realized that she'd missed a turn because she was caught up in such random musings as she walked along. She made a rough guess and took a path that ran in the general direction of Section B, Building H, Room #312. She saw a bicycle lying on its side, with a Masked Rider's mask attached to it. Nearby was a paper box of cookies that had been tossed there. Three children approached, and one picked up the box. There must have been some cookies left inside, because he began gobbling up something, like a stray dog. Another child suddenly ran off. He went up to the pile of cardboard boxes, empty bottles, and other rubbish that was next to an incinerator and began quickly sorting through it, by instinct. Finally he removed a certain cardboard box. He yanked with all his strength at its plastic lining. It wouldn't come loose. But he tore at the box relentlessly. What in the world did he intend to do with an ordinary piece of plastic? Ichiko wondered. When he finally got it, he let out a jubilant shriek. Carrying his loot in both arms, he dashed into the entrance of a building.

"It's the same thing," Ichiko murmured.

As she walked, over and over she came across children coming home from elementary school. Why was she so fascinated with children? The catalyst must have been that girl. Ichiko saw seven or eight children wearing satchels on their backs shout and begin to run. She stared hard at the single girl mixed in among the boys, wondering if it might possibly be her. The group sprang on a flower bed that someone had planted in an empty plot. They ripped up all the yellow daffodils and scampered off, disappearing behind a building.

It's the same thing.

She was gradually beginning to understand.

As it turned out, no one had been home at Room #312, Building H, Section B, the apartment with the nameplate Yoshimura. The door hadn't been locked, and it could be opened and closed freely. Ichiko had inquired of a person whom she happened to meet, and she learned that the old woman lived alone. There was no girl or anyone else living with her.

But she definitely went in there. I saw her. Ichiko had thought this over and over as she was walking back.

The train stopped at the next station and the other seat of the compartment in which those two brothers were sitting became available. When the mother began to move there, the younger boy quickly slipped into it. The mother settled for the seat where he'd been sitting until then. Ichiko and the boy ended up facing each other. Evidently he'd schemed so it would turn out that way.

The boy sat looking at a picture book, his gaze lowered. But Ichiko noticed that he didn't turn the pages at all. He was apparently conscious of Ichiko, because she kept staring at him. The older boy was wearing a gray suit with a red necktie, but a sport shirt was slightly visible under the younger boy's navy blue outfit. At first he'd turned around again and again to look at her, but apparently he'd decided to abandon the ploy of turning around. He now seemed to be pondering, with his eyes cast down on the picture book, how to take full advantage of the seating arrangement that he'd brought about. Inside that youthful head, a full-fledged sense of self-respect was operating. The boy seemed to be trying not to glance inadvertently at Ichiko, a woman. That effort was apparently making him a bit tense. His lowered gaze at times darted up, slid along the floor of the aisle toward Ichiko, and just before it reached her seat, quickly slid back.

After a while the mother took a Thermos from a large bag and poured juice into a paper cup. The younger boy raised his eyes in order to take the paper cup that was being handed to him. Right then, as if he'd at last obtained his opportunity, he stole a glance at Ichiko. He tossed a quick smile toward her, like a flash. At that moment the paper cup dropped to his knees and the juice splashed.

"Makio's a naughty boy. He doesn't hold his cup properly." The mother's voice carried all the way to Ichiko. She took out a large white handkerchief and briskly wiped the boy's knees.

Makio. *Which Chinese characters does he use to write his name?* Ichiko wondered.

"Such bad manners. Shame on you. It's because you're looking somewhere else."

At the words "looking somewhere else" Ichiko reacted, and simultaneously, the boy seemed to react. This time, not a smile but a conspiratorial glance was suddenly cast her way. The boy's glance and Ichiko's glance met, as if assuring each other that the mother had no idea where "somewhere else" was. Still, Ichiko didn't even smile. At first, she'd just once signaled him by smiling, but after that she had kept a perfectly straight face. The trivial slip had made the boy daring.

Although he was in the position of being observed directly by his mother and older brother, he devised one opportunity after another to glance at Ichiko. If he looked straight ahead he could see her, but he would absolutely not do so. Instead, he kept his eyes lowered on his picture book and waited for chances. For instance, when his brother began talking to him, or when he moved his body while making a big yawn, he would steal a glance at Ichiko with feigned nonchalance. But his trick of sneaking furtive glances while pretending not to was betrayed by the look in his eyes, which was growing more and more flirtatious. He would deliberately flutter his eyelashes. The upturned lashes were like a girl's.

For over an hour, Ichiko and the boy continued that game, but at length the boy hit upon something even more brazen. He came walking down the aisle toward Ichiko, heading toward the bathroom. When, as she'd expected, he brushed right by her shoulder, he gave her a seductive look. Just then, Ichiko detected a milky, babyish fragrance. The incongruity between that fragrance and the amorous glance gave the glance a surreal quality.

If at a moment like this Ichiko were to say something like, "How old are you, honey?" it would spoil everything. If she did that, she would instantly lapse into an ordinary woman who loved children. Nothing could be less erotic than a woman chatting to a youngster with a twinkle in her eye. As a matter of fact, Ichiko wasn't the least bit fond of children.

Where did you go today?

You and your brother are good pals, aren't you.

Where in Tokyo do you live?

The abnormally tense atmosphere that had developed during this past hour was like fragile crystal; just one such remark would shatter it. From somewhere, rays of light were shining on the myriad surfaces of that crystal, creating rainbowlike hues. No one else in the train car saw that. It was so subtle as to be nearly imperceptible. Until the boy had boarded the train, Ichiko had never imagined such a thing, and until now, she'd never encountered it. Even if she wanted sometime, somewhere, to find it again, it seemed unlikely that she would be able to; it was something that barely existed. Because of the boy, something bewitching was gradually coming to life in this car. Ichiko's role was simply to bear witness; that was all.

As the afternoon sunlight streaming through the window accumulated, the temperature in the car gradually rose, and Ichiko became drowsy. Everything began to glitter, as if mica fragments were swirling around, and Ichiko realized that she was slipping into a dream with her eyes wide open. But she could see the other people in the car and she could hear the rumbling of the train wheels, so she knew that she wasn't sleeping.

That girl Yoshimura Ruriko and the boy in this train called Makio were gracefully dancing together. It wasn't a ballroom dance or a folk dance. It rather resembled that melancholy, monotonous kind of dancing that Ichiko had seen in movies, done by noble men and women in royal palaces in the West.

Around the dancing couple, little children, like their attendants, were dancing—the boy who'd broken the window of her apartment with a rock, the child in the supermarket who'd been shrieking in some strange language, the boy who'd roughly torn up the cardboard box at the huge apartment complex, the elementary school pupils who'd ripped up the daffodils and run off, like a pack of stray dogs.

All together the children softly chanted, "Hoooh." Then, in the center of the circle of dancers, a flame appeared that looked crimson, yet transparent. Evidently the breath that each child had exhaled was transformed into that flame.

That's foxfire, Ichiko thought; then she awakened from her dream.

She couldn't decide if it was a good dream or a bad dream. Something sinister was lurking deep within it.

The boy was standing in front of his mother's seat. He was having the wool vest that he was wearing between his jacket and his sport shirt taken off by her. He'd probably begun to perspire because the car had become so warm. After his vest was taken off, his jacket was put on him again. He was surrendering his body to his mother's adept hands, like a helpless tyke. But over her shoulder, he was casting flirtatious glances at Ichiko, as if his eyes alone had briefly escaped from the role of the well-behaved boy.

ONE DAY ICHIKO was passing by the wig counter on her way to the stockroom. When she reached the large pillar that separated that counter from the one just before it, she sensed something gold glittering at the edge of her peripheral vision. Mixed in with the black and the chestnut-colored wigs were several blonde ones. Those sparkled even more than the others.

Ichiko looked in that direction and saw four or five women standing in front of the mirror trying on wigs. Sure enough, among them was that girl. The other time it had been a chestnut-colored wig, but today she had a blond one on her head. The hair was rather long, and it hung to her shoulders. She was examining herself in the mirror from this angle and that. As before, she radiated an allure that she herself didn't possess, no doubt thanks to the wig. Or had something that normally lay dormant within the girl been coaxed out by the wig? Even her shabby clothing seemed to glimmer with gold dust.

Again, the girl noticed Ichiko. She looked straight at her. She and Ichiko gazed defiantly at each other, but this time, unlike before, the girl's gaze bore steadily down on Ichiko's. Finally, in her elegant coiffure, the girl flashed a supremely confident smile at Ichiko.

"That won't work with me," Ichiko murmured.

As if dodging something dangerous, she passed, pretending not to have noticed the girl.

"If you want it that much, go ahead and take it," Ichiko said quietly.

When she passed the wig counter on her way back from the stockroom, the girl was no longer there. The blond wig, which Ichiko had been sure she'd steal, was on a mannequin's head.

She could almost see Yoshimura Ruriko's face there, superimposed on it.

The Suspended Bridge

Haruyo was walking quickly amid the droves of pedestrians. Even though she was tall, she'd always worn high-heeled shoes. She liked the sensation of her snugly encased toes firmly tapping the pavement as she moved lightly forward. People had even complimented her on her elegant gait. When she trotted along, the supple leather of her shoes flexing with each step, she felt as if she were still young. Today Haruyo was walking more briskly than usual. She was in a rush. She had stayed out longer than she'd expected on her errand, so her children were probably restlessly awaiting her return.

"Oh!" Haruyo uttered a little cry, and immediately she sensed someone amid the crowd streaming past her in the opposite direction utter the same cry. Both she and the other person were walking quickly, so they both came to a sharp stop in the middle of the pedestrian crosswalk, like cars that had suddenly slammed on their brakes.

The other person took several steps back. It was Matsuyama Iwao. Thirteen years had passed since the two of them had graduated from the same university. Soon after graduating they had met on three occasions, but then Matsuyama had been transferred to an office outside the Tokyo area and Haruyo had heard no more about him after that. She'd completely lost touch with all her other friends from those days as well. Actually, Haruyo herself had deliberately severed those ties.

"You must be back at the head office," said Haruyo, glancing over Matsuyama, who seemed to have filled out a bit since the old days. As she gazed at him, memories from the past seemed about to seep forth from him, like a foul odor. Around his face, the faces of her former companions began to appear, like pictures that had been drawn in invisible ink. As the two of them stood there, on both sides of them droves of people returning home from their jobs streamed past incessantly. A voice inside Haruyo murmured, *Don't keep standing here. Plunge into this stream of people and be swept along.* Maybe it was her body's self-protective instinct.

"*He's* back too. Did you know? Oh, you did know," said Matsuyama.

Haruyo's impulse to disappear into the crowd had perhaps been prompted by a visceral realization of what Matsuyama was about to say. Caught off-guard by his remark, she'd been stunned. Matsuyama had misinterpreted her blank stare to mean that she already knew.

"No, I didn't know. Not at all." Haruyo lowered her voice when she said this.

He—Igawa Toshiaki.

During her childhood Haruyo had occasionally dreamed of a suspended bridge. She didn't know why she would have dreamed of such a thing. She'd probably actually crossed such a bridge only once or twice, on school outings. She couldn't remember when or where. The bridge, which consisted of only rope and wooden planks, was suspended over a gorge deep in the mountains. It swayed precariously as she stood in the middle of it. When she looked down, she was gripped by the sensation that something demonic had just whooshed by. After that, she became aware of an infinite void stretching beneath her, where she could fall forever without reaching the bottom. These were feelings that she'd actually experienced. But her dream included another sensation. In her dream she had an ominous feeling that she herself was on the verge of helplessly dissolving. That self was standing in the middle of a suspended bridge, gazing up at the blue sky. Beneath her lay a fiery abyss. Somewhere a bird seemed to be crying, "Look out! Look out!" The sensation was both harrowing and delightful. Unable to decide whether it would be better to cross the bridge and set foot on solid ground or to let herself fall into the fiery abyss, she lost all sense of judgment and simply stood rocking back and forth on the bridge. For some reason, those dreams she'd had from time to time as a child now sprang to mind.

"What's wrong? Maybe I shouldn't have mentioned it," Matsuyama said teasingly. Then he pulled his wallet from his breast pocket and removed a business card from it. He tapped the card with his fingertip, saying that this was his office, and handed it to her.

"What you just told me—is it true?" asked Haruyo, glancing at the place on Matsuyama's business card where his title was printed. It read, "XX Trading Company, Tokyo Headquarters, Sales Section #2, Assistant Section Head."

Matsuyama took the card back from Haruyo, removed a ballpoint pen from his breast pocket, and scribbled some numbers on the back of the card.

"He's there. *He*. You know who I mean by *he*. But maybe it was wrong of me. Should I have kept quiet about it?" In Matsuyama's face, which seemed to have filled out a bit since the old days, suddenly the eyes twinkled amiably.

The signal changed and the two of them spontaneously dashed off, in different directions. From left and right, cars began streaming toward the place where the two of them had stood gazing at the past that glowed like a ruby. Haruyo glanced back, and for an instant she had the illusion that that precious red jewel was being crushed beneath the tires of the cars that raced past, one after another. Then she noticed that Matsuyama was standing on the sidewalk across the street and waving to her.

The entire city had turned into a bridge that was swaying back and forth, suspended beneath the yellowish twilight sky.

Haruyo looked at the back of the business card and saw figures written on it that evidently comprised a phone number: 587–22XX.

She stood motionless on the sidewalk. She was savoring her awareness of another self that had suddenly emerged from within her. This self was different from the self that until minutes before had been rushing to get home as soon as possible for the sake of the children, who were waiting for their dinner. Rather, this self was rejecting that other self. Haruyo's entire body was saying, "No."

She felt terribly unbalanced. She wanted to crouch down on the sidewalk lest her body collapse. She recalled how long ago, time and again she had wanted to crouch down, heedless of where she was, just as she did now.

Haruyo looked around her. This enormous city, these throngs returning home from work, this huge conglomeration of buildings, these countless shops. How strange it was. That even though these myriad people and things were teeming around her, there was no connection between any of them and what was now happening inside her. Haruyo felt as if she were all alone in some place like an air pocket. And how strange it was that that single phrase uttered by Matsuyama Iwao could shake her to her roots; she felt like a plant that had been torn out of the ground.

"*Passion*," murmured Haruyo. Something that could only be called *passion* was tingling inside her.

Haruyo stared again at the back of the business card that she was pinching between her thumb and index finger, as if she were holding an explosive by the edge. She silently pronounced to herself the numbers scrawled on it: 587–22XX.

Numbers that could connect her to the past, if this moment she were to dial them on a red public phone. Numbers that had the power to again thrust open the door to the past that she herself had firmly closed.

He—Igawa Toshiaki.

Like a violent intruder, the past had invaded the present. It was as if Matsuyama Iwao had knocked Haruyo down, then strode across the street.

There was a thing called *passion* that could only lead to self-destruction if you came in contact with it. Or rather, lodged deep within this world was a mineral vein called *passion*. Unless a person happened to come in touch with that, she'd probably spend her entire life unaware of its existence. If Haruyo herself hadn't met Igawa Toshiaki, she would probably never have experienced it. Neither her husband nor any other man had ever given her access to that precious mineral lode.

"*Passion*," Haruyo murmured and began walking slowly along.

If you touched that, you couldn't tear yourself away from it, and eventually it would destroy you. But even if you managed to distance yourself from that, it wasn't as if it disappeared. Its hot, dark energy continued to smolder deep within this world. It wasn't simply available to whoever desired it. But it could invigorate a woman's life if the right man served as a conduit.

When Haruyo arrived home, her children rushed at her, squealing excitedly. She was shocked at herself for feeling a revulsion toward them that she'd never felt before.

"DO WATCH OUT for reckless drivers, dear," said Haruyo as she saw Eizō off in front of the gate. It was the first time that she'd ever said such a thing.

"Yeah, I don't want to end up like Gōkichi. But there's no chance of that." Eizō made this reference to Haruyo's younger brother, who had died in a traffic accident, as he repeatedly pulled the hinge of the iron gate with his fingers.

"Heaven forbid. Last night I woke up in the middle of the night and thought, what would become of me if anything were to happen to you." Again Haruyo made an uncharacteristic remark.

"Even if someone somewhere lays a trap for me, I won't be caught. I have a knack for avoiding harm, even in risky situations. I've always been that way." Eizō had a habit of saying that he'd always land on his feet. As he spoke, he bent down to examine the hinge.

"That's not what I mean. If you suddenly died, I'd be at a total loss." Haruyo felt herself becoming more and more agitated as she spoke.

"It's starting to give way. I'll change it this Sunday. Tell the kids to be careful. If this heavy gate fell down on them it would be a disaster." Eizō clapped his hands together to shake off the rust that had stuck to them.

"It's you who should be careful. If you're hit by a car when you're coming home today, it would be terrible. Or tomorrow. Or the day after tomorrow." Haruyo made her final untypical remark and scrutinized Eizō.

From the second-floor window the children called out, "Papa! Papa!" Eizō waved in their direction. Then, just as usual, he began striding down the road in front of the gate.

"Ah, such an unimaginative man," murmured Haruyo as she watched Eizō's back recede into the distance. His sturdy back was dependable, like a blunt weapon. Inside that body stretched a network of practical nerves, so that even if someone somewhere laid a trap for him, he wouldn't be ensnared by it. But one could say that he hadn't a single "impractical" nerve in his body. He was a person who never reflected on why he was here, or why his wife was here.

Last night Haruyo had awakened in the middle of the night when something that felt like a painful memory had welled up from the depths of her dream. She had wondered what would become of her if she suddenly lost her husband. Since getting married, she'd never once considered such a thing, nor had she ever said such a thing to Eizō.

Why hadn't he been struck by the strangeness of her uncharacteristic remarks?

As she puzzled over this, Haruyo began walking after Eizō, who was heading down the road toward the bus stop. She glanced back at the second floor of their home and saw that the children's faces were no longer at the window. The flower-patterned curtain was drenched in morning light and looked terribly white.

"I'll keep you company, dear," said Haruyo when she caught up to Eizō.

"Isn't it too early for the supermarket?" Eizō didn't slacken his pace.

"It's not that; I just felt like walking with you like this." Haruyo managed a slightly coquettish smile.

"Oh, really?"

"Don't I seem a bit strange to you this morning?" Haruyo went straight to the heart of the matter.

Eizō stopped, pulled out a cigarette, put it in his mouth, and lit it. "Hmmm."

"Oh dear, there's a hair." Haruyo picked a strand of hair off Eizō's left shoulder. She felt as if she had picked up an alien substance. She'd been familiar with Eizō's hair for twelve years, and yet she felt that way about it. At the same time, she found herself fondly recalling the sense of intimacy she'd felt with another man's hair. That hair was always freshly shampooed and gave off a pleasant fragrance of pomade. Comb marks that formed a precise pattern were visible in it, and the stiff, short black hair was seldom disarrayed.

The scent of that pomade came back to Haruyo now. In the crisp spring morning air, the voluptuous atmosphere of the past trembled like a flame.

"I'm strange, aren't I?" said Haruyo, as if trying to get a rise out of Eizō. The two of them were walking toward the bus stop like a happily married couple. It was the road that Haruyo took every morning when she walked her older child to kindergarten, but it was two hours earlier than that, and the position of the morning sun was making the road look brand new.

"I can't concern myself with a person's every whim, you know."

"Do you mean with *my* whims?"

"No, with anyone's whims. That's so, Haruyo, that's just the way it is."

"What's the way it is?"

"The only sure things are what you can see with your eyes."

"But today, don't you think I'm different from usual? Look—as you can see with your eyes, I'm walking with you like this to the bus stop."

"Relax. You're the same as ever," said Eizō, expelling a stream of smoke into the morning air.

Haruyo couldn't tell if the feeling that came over her was one of resignation or despair. Although she'd been totally transformed since yesterday, her husband didn't even notice. Haruyo suddenly resolved to make an effort the next day and the day after that to get her husband to take notice of her. It was a peculiar sort of effort. Because if he did notice, it would create a problem for her. But Haruyo wanted to see if she could make even a small crack in her husband's attitude, which was like a brick wall.

And yet, how much she depended on this very kind of person, Haruyo mused as she walked along with Eizō down the road to the bus stop. It was just this sort of husband who cherished Haruyo's outer self and was oblivious to her inner self, who shielded her from that passion that seemed on the verge of burning her. If today her husband were suddenly to die in a traffic accident, she would surely turn into a seething current of desire and rush pell-mell toward the phone number she'd received yesterday from Matsuyama Iwao.

After she'd seen off Eizō, Haruyo felt like going to see the ocean. When she said that to her children, the older one insisted on staying home from kindergarten. Haruyo ended up taking both of them. Since yesterday the children's shrill voices had been getting on her nerves. She would stop by her family home and leave the children with her mother, who lived alone there. She wanted to be by herself as soon as possible and gaze at the ocean. She wanted to stand alone on the shore of the Shōnan Coast, where she'd gone to swim every summer of her girlhood with her parents and brother.

After Haruyo had returned home yesterday, her children and husband had been there the whole time and she hadn't been able to be alone for a moment. When her insides had flamed and churned and risen up to her mouth; when her whole body had felt elated, as if she were walking on air; when she'd felt rootless and distraught, as if she'd been spirited away, even though she'd never left the spot; what torture it had been to behave just as usual—to prepare dinner, keep the conversation going at the table, and thoughtfully respond to each question that the children had fired at her. She wanted to be alone as soon as possible. She wanted to confront herself in solitude.

Today Haruyo felt too shaky to drive, so she decided to go by taxi to Tokyo Station, then go the rest of the way by train.

In the taxi the radio was blaring. It was tuned to a personal advice program. Haruyo's ears were assailed by the voice of a middle-aged woman who was lamenting that her inability to pay her debts was casting a pall over her life, and there was no solution but to commit suicide. When that conversation ended, what sounded like the voice of another middle-aged woman began stammeringly to relate the woman's anguish over her husband's philandering. The circumstances were evidently a bit different from ordinary infidelity. The husband and wife loved each other. And yet the husband also loved other women. He insisted on carrying on numerous affairs quite openly.

"He's like a monster. A love monster. I realize I'm talking about my own husband." This is what the woman said.

"How do you want to resolve the problem?" the male program host asked.

The woman remained silent.

"Do you want to find some way of keeping your husband faithful to you? Or else, do you want to work toward an advantageous divorce settlement?" The program host tried to guide the woman.

The woman remained silent.

"Whichever you choose, the important thing is to make a decision. To go on like this is agony for you. Come, now. Try to verbalize your wishes. Once I know what you want, I think I'll be able to advise you."

"I'll kill him."

"What's that?! Ma'am . . . !"

"I *have* killed him. Already."

"Excuse me, will you please turn off the radio?" Haruyo said to the driver.

As soon as the radio noise ceased, the children began making a racket.

Maybe she'd misunderstood the last thing the woman had said. Haruyo regretted making the driver turn off the radio before she'd verified that.

When she looked outside the car window, the familiar Tokyo scenery seemed to be portending something. Until yesterday, the city had simply been an extension of the comfortable nook where Haruyo had been leading her life. But now the entire city was tinged with an ambiance that was at once terrifying and intimate, because Igawa Toshiaki was breathing the air here.

"So he's back from America," murmured Haruyo.

How different the scenery appeared, depending on whether one knew or didn't know that a certain man was living in the same city! That difference depended not on whether or not the man was there, but on whether or not one knew that he was there. Haruyo's past, which had been buried alive, had revived. The city panorama, pregnant with memories and expectations, seemed to be bursting with vitality, like a living creature, and surrounded by a halo of light. Haruyo narrowed her eyes, as if protecting them from dazzling sunlight, and gazed at it.

"Mama, you say we're going to the ocean, but *where* on the ocean do you mean?" The older child, a girl, had been asking the same thing over and over from a little while before.

"Maamaa, Maamaa, Maamaa," the younger child, a boy, kept bleating, like a talking baby doll.

"*Why* are we going to see the ocean? *Why*, Mama? It's not even summertime. *Why*? *Why*?" the girl persisted.

Haruyo kept staring intently out the car window. The throbbing of Igawa Toshiaki's heart seemed to be emanating from somewhere in the city landscape.

"Mama, you're different from usual," her daughter said in a shrill voice, then burst into tears. "Scary. You're scary, Mama," she said between sobs.

"Scaary, scaary," parroted the little boy.

Haruyo pretended not to hear anything, despite the din.

Suddenly the voice of the woman on the personal advice program came back to her. Haruyo was seized by a delusion that she herself, distressed over debts, was now rushing toward the ocean, intent on committing suicide with her two young children. At a time like that, the children of a woman who just kept staring at a figment of her imagination would no doubt respond sensitively, and cry out, "Scary! Mama's scary!" At a time like that, the ocean that lay beyond the woman's gaze would probably be a rough, chilly gray ocean that tossed up waves that looked like rows of bared white teeth. But now, Haruyo was picturing a different kind of ocean. Desires that had been lying submerged deep within that ocean had risen, and they were floating like oil across its entire surface, making the water glisten with all the colors of the rainbow.

AT LAST, HARUYO SAID TO HERSELF when she was alone in her own room on the second floor of her parents' home.

She removed that business card from her handbag as if she were removing an explosive. She held it in her right hand and stared intently at it. She scrutinized that phone number. Was it Igawa's office or his home number? Matsuyama Iwao had said, "There's where he is," so it was probably his office number.

Spring sunlight floated languidly outside the window. The garden was large, so the house next door wasn't visible from here. Only the bright sky appeared, like a square mounted within the window frame. The water in the garden pond cast a reflection on the ceiling that trembled and glimmered like a heat wave.

Haruyo suddenly stood up. Perhaps partly because she was on the second floor and partly because of this effulgence, she had the sensation of being on a suspended bridge. She wanted to grasp something real, rather than being suspended in midair, so she began slowly descending the stairs. At the foot of the stairs was the front hall, where there was a phone. Haruyo dialed the number: 03–485–12XX. No, she could never have done this at her own home. She felt as if she'd returned to her family home today not to see the ocean but to use the telephone here.

"Hello." Sure enough, it was a man's voice.

For some reason, Haruyo's heart didn't continue to thump. Instead, her insides became eerily quiet, and that stillness seemed to cause her chest muscles to constrict painfully.

"Uh," Haruyo stammered.

"XX Trading Company, Sales Division, Section Two," the voice continued.

Haruyo was confused.

"Oh, this is Mr. Matsuyama, isn't it. Matsuyama Iwao." She immediately realized that she'd dialed the wrong number. Her distress yielded to amusement and she felt immensely relieved. The mere thought that Igawa Toshiaki might actually have answered the phone made her shudder. Just what had she intended to say to Igawa after all these years, anyway?

"Oh, Haruyo, I'm so sorry about yesterday. I'm feeling terrible about it," said Matsuyama. From his tone of voice, Haruyo imagined that he might be bowing in front of the telephone.

"Don't be silly." This was how Haruyo responded.

Both of them remained silent for a moment. Haruyo waited for Matsuyama to begin speaking.

"Well, I hope you don't think I was out of line."

"Was that how my face looked?"

"Well, sort of."

"What do you mean, 'sort of'?"

"Well, frankly, you looked so aghast that I was startled."

"Really?!" said Haruyo, trying not to shriek. She thought that maybe now, too, her face looked aghast.

People assume they are always wearing the facial expression that they think of as their characteristic expression. They're convinced that the face they see in the mirror in the morning is the one they are still wearing at noon. And when they meet someone and have a conversation, they're sure that they are making the same face they saw in the mirror that morning.

Haruyo recalled reading something like this in an old fable. One day, a woman tormented by passion peered into a river, and on the water's surface, the face of a demon appeared. The woman went around telling people that she'd seen a demon in the river. She didn't realize that it was her own face reflected in the water.

A female demon is no mere fanciful creature. Under certain circumstances, an ordinary woman can turn into a demon in an instant. She may even sprout horns. Her eyes may slant way up and turn golden. Her face may look as if it's about to catch fire. There's nothing extraordinary about a human face doing such things.

That's right, back in those days. . . . Haruyo was on the verge of remembering something about a demon.

"About Igawa . . ." Matsuyama Iwao said.

"Why did he come back from America?" Haruyo interrupted what she was about to recall and returned to the present moment.

"There was some sort of mess at the embassy in Washington. He'd risen to First Secretary, but he came back to the Ministry of Foreign Affairs. He's been here since last year."

"What sort of a mess, I wonder?"

"Nothing that involved a woman, so you can relax."

"Oh, he's not the type of man who would let an affair with a woman turn into a public scandal. Never. Not in a million years. No matter how many women he was involved with, on the surface he'd be poised and in control. He's that sort of man, cold as ice," said Haruyo, Igawa's impeccably groomed figure floating in her mind's eye.

"Come, now, Haruyo, lighten up. It was ages ago, after all," said Matsuyama, then he chuckled and hung up.

Then what she'd been about to recall erupted like lava from a volcano. Haruyo snatched up her mother's cigarettes, which had been left on the step in the front hall, and started up to the room upstairs.

"Mama, aren't we going to the ocean?"

"Maamaa, Maamaa."

The children's pesky voices pursued Haruyo from the foot of the stairs.

Haruyo stood on the second-floor landing and looked down at her children. Until yesterday, when she'd heard about Igawa Toshi-aki, she had lavished such affection on them. She was aware of how indifferent she felt toward them now. They looked like a pair of bothersome beasts that she'd never seen before.

When a man comes into a woman's life, maternal feelings go out the window, Haruyo mused.

"Maama's a liar, Maama's a liar," chanted the children in unison.

Haruyo entered the room that she'd been in before. There she surrendered to her memories.

Fourteen or fifteen years ago, when she was at university, she and her friends would sometimes have a dance party. One day she and Igawa had met before going to a party that began in the evening.

In those days Haruyo would go to meet Igawa as if she were being drawn into an inferno. Her body would burn like a torch. It would blaze up the way a pine tree, when ignited, spurts into an erect, vigorous flame because of the resin in it. When she was with Igawa, anything contradictory, anything excessive, anything vague, anything inadequate ceased to exist. She was in an inferno, but it was where she belonged. Her entire body felt sure of this as the hours with Igawa passed blissfully. He would take her to a first-class hotel where ordinarily students didn't stay. He would reserve the room for the night, but they would never spend the night there. He would transform the place into an inferno, but that atmosphere would absolutely never extend beyond that room. After leaving there they would drink tea in the hotel lobby, and Igawa would turn into a very cantankerous young man. "Your lipstick is smudged; go to the bathroom and fix it." "Don't fidget; bad manners show the ugly side of human nature." "The color of your outfit and your handbag don't match. I'm embarrassed to be seen with a girl who wears odd clothes." These are the kinds of remarks he would make to her in the lobby. Even though he was the same age as Haruyo, his way of speaking was like a middle-aged gentleman's. Somehow, that suited him very well.

Just before the dance party that evening, she and Igawa were drinking tea in the lobby, as usual.

"You have some cologne, don't you?"

"I have three or four kinds that my father bought me on trips abroad."

"I'm asking if you have any with you right now."

"Why?"

"We're going to a dance party. I'm sure you know what I mean."

"Oh, I'm sorry!"

"If I dance once with a woman who has body odor, I won't dance with her again."

Until meeting Igawa, Haruyo had been told by many men that no woman could match her in beauty of face and figure, or in refinement. But when confronted with Igawa's perversity, she was made to feel like a country milkmaid.

After leaving the lobby, they got in Igawa's car and he drove, maintaining a sullen silence. He was a different man from the one who had been so ardent in the hotel room. It was typical of him to suddenly turn sullen on these occasions. But Haruyo was probably more painfully aware of it that day because his affection in the hotel room had been extraordinary. The contrast between those hours and the present utterly bewildered her.

At the dance party, Igawa didn't choose Haruyo to be his partner, but another girl. Haruyo didn't know her. When one song ended and the next began, Igawa danced with that girl again. Haruyo was baffled as to why Igawa was treating her this way. It felt to her like sheer meanness. A little while before, her body had become a flaming torch; that memory was still fresh, and it twisted painfully within her. Her innards twisted over and over. The embers of a blazing fire were embedded in that pain.

Haruyo felt as if she were now reliving that scene that had occurred fourteen or fifteen years before. She'd snatched her mother's cigarettes from downstairs, and she smoked, for the first time in a long while. She'd begun smoking when she was trying to bring herself to part from Igawa. During that time she'd happened to receive a marriage proposal that pleased her mother, and she had leaped at it. After that, she quit smoking completely, but she still associated the taste of cigarettes with the taste of passion.

While she was at that dance party, Haruyo had quietly gotten up and gone to the bathroom. She looked in the mirror there and saw that her own face had turned into a demon's. Her face powder had become terribly blotchy. Perhaps it was because she'd applied her makeup hastily before leaving the hotel room, or else because Igawa's metamorphosis had made her begin perspiring profusely.

Her metallic-looking eyes appeared to be slanting upward and her hair standing on end.

It's not that the female demon described in Japanese legends actually exists. The ordinary, perfectly normal woman, under certain circumstances and at certain moments, can turn into one. Anyone who saw this happen would probably let out a shriek. Only the woman who saw it happen to herself would know why she'd turned into a demon.

How many times had Haruyo turned into a demon during her affair with Igawa Toshiaki? As long as she was involved with Igawa, she would sometimes be forced to turn into a demon. Finally, she could no longer stand being such a woman.

There are men who turn women into demons. A tender, passionate man is more apt to do so than any other kind of man. A man like that will fling a woman out of a fiery crucible onto a stony wasteland. Whether he does so intentionally or not is impossible for the woman to tell. When that type of man is alone with a woman, he always becomes a tender man who makes her burn with desire. It's not that he's a rogue or a playboy. But the woman has to agonize over the man's façade of sincerity. She won't know whether or not he's truly sincere. The man's façade is flawless.

"DEAR," HARUYO CALLED to her husband, who was in the bed next to hers. Light from the garden lamp seeped through a crack in the wooden rain shutters and pierced the darkness. Haruyo called in a gradually louder and louder voice until Eizō woke up.

"Do you love me?" asked Haruyo, uncharacteristically.

Rather than hoping for a response, she was hoping Eizō might notice that there was something unusual about her.

"Why did you marry me?" she asked, something she'd never asked him before. Since Haruyo had rushed blindly into a marriage that her mother had encouraged, it hadn't been necessary to press her partner to reveal his feelings.

"Because you were prettier than any other woman," replied Eizō. If another man said this, it would sound like mere flattery, but when Eizō spoke the line it sounded as if he were stating a fact.

"You're right. I *was* pretty," said Haruyo. And yet, Igawa Toshiaki had sometimes transformed that pretty woman into a demon, she thought. Haruyo suddenly felt like talking about men who transform pretty women into demons.

"You know Okamura Masako, don't you?" she began.

"Who's that?" said Eizō, as Haruyo had expected.

"Don't you know? She's a friend of mine from my college days, although I haven't seen her in ages," said Haruyo. Okamura Masako was just a fictitious name that she'd blurted out.

"I don't remember her. Did she come to our wedding?" Eizō asked, taking Haruyo seriously.

"The other day I happened to run into her. She steered me into a coffee shop and poured out her heart to me. She'd been happily married, when last year an old sweetheart of hers returned from abroad. Okamura Masako is a beautiful woman. But she said that in the past, when she was with this man, she would sometimes turn into a demon."

"Haruyo, I'll listen to the rest of this story on Saturday night, or whenever. Just look at the time—it's two in the morning." Eizō's tone of voice sounded like he was pointing with his finger, so Haruyo turned to look at the bedside table, and saw that the luminous dial on the clock indeed read five past two.

"Saturday night? We can't take our own sweet time like that. Okamura Masako is beside herself. I have to give her some advice."

"Well, I'll leave it to you to think of something of tell her. I'm no good at that sort of thing."

The two of them fell silent, so the darkness seemed to deepen.

"Dear, do you love me?" Haruyo asked again.

"That's got nothing to do with this. I'm saying that I don't want to hear about your friend's predicament right now. Don't you understand?" said Eizō, and he turned away from her to try to sleep.

Why doesn't this man notice the change that's come over me? Haruyo said to herself.

"I wonder if he really loves me," she ventured.

Exhausted from grappling with Igawa Toshiaki's façade, Haruyo had married Eizō, who seemed to be a paragon of sincerity. But what, in fact, was at the core of Eizō's sincerity?

"So you married me because I was pretty? Yes, I suppose so. Is my outer appearance all that matters to you? Obviously it is." Haruyo prattled on to herself.

"Just this morning you said that, didn't you—the only sure things are what you can see with your eyes." Now genuinely irate, Haruyo scratched Eizō's skin. That skin was like the leather of a chair that had become thoroughly familiar to her from years of use.

"Things you can see are like objects, aren't they? They're like objects," Haruyo went on. At the same time, she wondered if she'd ever actually glimpsed inside Eizō, whose skin was like the leather of a leather chair.

"It's futile to try to grasp something that you can't see. You make do with what you can see. You make do. That's the essence of wisdom, Haruyo," said Eizō, his back still turned to her.

Well, now, he's quite the philosopher. I didn't think he had it in him to say such things, Haruyo mused.

"Oh, I must do something to help out Okamura Masako. Dear, you say such sensible things. Won't you think of something to tell Masako? She was talking about the difference between sincerity and a façade of sincerity. She said that her ex-lover's façade of sincerity had nearly driven her mad. And she relied on her husband's sincerity, and she felt secure, and was content."

As Haruyo spoke, she was thinking that when you desperately tried to grasp the inner essence of something that you could see, but you only encountered a façade so you settled for what you could see, maybe you'd think that you had grasped something genuine. And yet, maybe the genuineness she sensed in Eizō was nothing more than the genuineness possessed by a leather chair.

Why isn't this man shaken by anything? I have to try to make him aware of my inner self, Haruyo said to herself.

She thought it strange to test her husband like this now, after having been contentedly married for twelve years. It was as if she were plunging into her husband the dagger that she ought to have plunged into Igawa.

The sound of snoring came from the bed next to hers. Haruyo was conscious of herself lying alone in the depths of the darkness. From that position, she was spying intently on the creature lying right beside her, although she couldn't see him. The length of his snore varied. Eizō was sleeping so soundly that, other than his snoring, he gave no sign of being alive.

Who the hell is Okamura Masako and where is she from?

If only Eizō had become more worked up, he would have shown more proof of being alive.

587–22XX, HARUYO DIALED. Until then, she'd been staring hard at the clock, watching the second-hand needle go around, for ten minutes. The other party answered in a heartbeat. Haruyo felt as if her heart had left her body and she was hearing it beat in midair.

"Ministry of Foreign Affairs, North America Division, First Section," said the voice on the other end of the line.

It was a terribly hoarse voice. Had Igawa Toshiaki come to possess such a voice? His voice had been low, but it had had a pleasant tone. As Haruyo recalled the voice from the past, she felt as if she were hearing her heartbeat come from a loudspeaker that was suspended in the air diagonally above her.

"Is that Mr. Igawa?" Because Haruyo was speaking with great effort, her voice sounded somewhat different from normal to her.

"Igawa isn't here today," said the other person.

"Hasn't he come back from Washington?" Haruyo ended up phrasing the question in this way.

"Who's calling, please?"

"Never mind. He's absent? Oh, I see . . ."

"I suppose he won't be here tomorrow, either."

"Why?"

The other person didn't respond. "Well, good-bye," said Haruyo, and she hung up.

She sank to the floor in front of the phone, feeling as if strength were draining from her entire body. She wondered how many times until now some trouble with Igawa had forced her to crouch down on the ground in distress. Before her lay a single pink slipper, turned inside out, that her daughter had tossed off before going to kindergarten.

"*Is that Mr. Igawa?*" Haruyo had asked thirteen years before.

"*Toshiaki isn't here now,*" said his mother, who had answered the phone.

"*Congratulations on his passing the exam for the Ministry of Foreign Affairs,*" Haruyo had said, pronouncing the words with every ounce of energy she could muster in order to match the mother's formal tone of voice.

"*Who's calling, please?*"

"*Never mind. Won't he be home today?*"

"*No, and I suppose he won't be here tomorrow, either.*"

"*Why?*"

Haruyo recalled the very similar phone conversation that she'd had thirteen years earlier.

During the hours when the two of them were apart, Igawa Toshiaki was the kind of man who had made Haruyo wonder what he was doing and when and where. Except when he'd temporarily alighted at the point in space occupied by Haruyo, how he spent his time was as misty to her as the sea of clouds that one sees from the window of an airplane. But if she'd dared to even gently inquire about his doings, he probably would have punished her by being incommunicado for two or three months. Once that actually had happened. At that time Haruyo had asked Matsuyama Iwao if Igawa was involved with a number of women. Matsuyama had replied that Igawa was busy associating with people who would be able to help him get ahead in the future. It had occurred to Haruyo that "associating" could be interpreted in a variety of ways. Later, Igawa had gone to Washington as an assistant diplomat right after marrying the daughter of a distinguished family; it was a perfect arrangement. Haruyo had never heard a single snide remark about the situation. But in that case, too, Haruyo was unable to perceive anything beyond the façade.

"I suppose he won't be here tomorrow, either."

"Why?"

Haruyo was vaguely reflecting on the phone conversation that she'd had twice—in the past and just now. What a relief it would have been to her if the other person had said something definite, such as "He'll be absent from work tomorrow, too," or "He won't be home tomorrow, either." Both the official at the Ministry of Foreign Affairs and Igawa's mother had spoken as if they were keeping a secret from Haruyo. Or perhaps Igawa withheld information about himself from his co-workers and his family, just as he did from Haruyo, so the official at the ministry and his mother could only speak in tentative terms.

Next, Haruyo felt compelled to dial another phone number.

"I phoned him," she said to Matsuyama Iwao.

"He's changed, hasn't he?" Matsuyama's unexpected words startled her.

"Changed? Do you really think he's someone who can change? A man like him can't possibly change. You can be sure that right now he's leading a picture-perfect life—fine wife, fine children, fine position. A man who never fails to present himself to others as cool and in control. He's an expert at that. It's his sole purpose in life." Haruyo blurted this out in one breath.

"His nerves seem pretty frazzled," said Matsuyama.

Haruyo was sprawled out on the floor beneath the phone, her toes fiddling with her daughter's pink slipper. She was making this risky phone call during the brief interval when her son was napping.

"Perfect family. Perfect love affairs." Haruyo went on as if she were talking to herself. Even now, after all these years, she couldn't blot out her mental image of Igawa dallying with dozens of women.

"No," mumbled Matsuyama.

"What? What do you know?" Haruyo felt as if blood had begun spurting from an old wound.

"Did he tell you anything?"

"Actually, he was absent."

"I might have known," said Matsuyama, sounding as if he were putting a cigarette into his mouth.

"What in the world is going on?"

"I just told you, didn't I? He seems to be exhausted somehow."

"He can skip work just because he's tired?"

"I don't know the details, but he's different from the old days. Maybe it's because he's turned into a typical bureaucrat, but he doesn't reveal himself at all. He was always that kind of guy, except with me, he didn't act that way. He just said one thing—'I'm tired.' Oh, he also said that the atmosphere in America seems basically different from Japan. That the amount of oxygen in the air seems to be different."

That was all Matsuyama said.

Haruyo was tossed into midair without having grasped anything certain. She felt as though the past had been like that, too. No matter how much she'd questioned Matsuyama, she hadn't been able to get a glimpse of Igawa's hidden self.

> Red, red balloon,
> I send you to the sky.
> Red, red balloon,
> You suddenly get wide.
> Red, red balloon,
> Up there you become
> Great big Mister Sun.

Her little boy had woken up. He was crawling down the stairs, chanting the verse in a singsong voice.

Haruyo looked out the window. Beyond the square frame, radiant light suffused the late-morning sky. Haruyo walked to the window and looked up. High in the hazy spring sky, a bright red balloon was rising.

THE DAYS PASSED, and Haruyo remained in a state of suspense. The man whom she had mustered her courage to phone, in hopes of dispelling that mood, had been mysteriously absent, so Haruyo couldn't bring herself to call again. She felt herself becoming more and more distressed.

One Sunday, Haruyo glanced at the newspaper that Eizō had left spread out on the kitchen table, which was bathed in the morning sunlight, and she gave a little cry. Under the headline TOP GOVERNMENT OFFICIAL COMMITS SUICIDE, the following article appeared.

> On April 14, at 4:22 P.M., a man jumped from the fifth floor of the XX Building near the Ministry of Foreign Affairs. His body was discovered by two deliverymen for the XX Transportation Company who were working in the street. The man who jumped has been identified as Igawa Toshiaki (age 36) of the North America Division, First Section, of the Ministry of Foreign Affairs. He died immediately, on impact. Mr. Igawa was sent as an assistant diplomat to the Japanese embassy in Washington, D.C. in 19XX. He returned to Japan last year to assume his current post. An elite government official who graduated from Tokyo University Law School, Igawa never deviated from his profession's so-called success track. As yet, no suicide note has been found.

"So he jumped off a building yesterday evening," Haruyo murmured to herself. Then a phantasmic scene took shape before her eyes, and she stood watching it, transfixed.

Her four-year-old son was standing at the base of a tall building, chanting over and over,

> Red, red balloon,
> I send you to the sky.
> Red, red balloon,
> You suddenly get wide.

The child gave the red balloon a poke and it floated in midair, like an object in a dream. Then the balloon began to rise lightly into the sky, as if the child's wishes were guiding it. A man who was exhausted for reasons unknown to anyone was walking alone in a deserted building that Saturday evening. The door of the fifth-floor emergency exit happened to be open, so he went out onto the landing and gazed at the sky above the city. He heard a childish, ghostly voice chanting, "Red, red balloon, I send you to the sky." He looked in the direction of the voice and saw a balloon that resembled the evening sun come floating up into the sky. The unearthly young voice kept on chanting, "Red, red balloon, you suddenly get wide." Suddenly the man was seized by a desire to become one with that wafting balloon, so he leaped toward it into space. Just then, the red balloon turned into the evening sun.

That's how people must commit suicide, mused Haruyo. "Dear," she called to her husband, who was in the garden, then she stepped out onto the veranda. That rainbow-colored sea of passion had come welling up from somewhere deep within the earth, and Haruyo was already immersed in it to her neck.

"What's wrong, Haruyo? Your face is crimson."

Eizō had turned to look at her, a large shovel in his hands. He was digging a hole in the corner of the garden to plant a gardenia that he'd bought the day before at a nursery.

"You remember Okamura Masako? She came here yesterday morning," Haruyo said impulsively.

A look of disgust flitted across Eizō's face. But he must have immediately suppressed his feelings, because in a moment his face reverted to its typical bland expression.

"My face is crimson?" Haruyo walked toward her husband through the grass in her stocking feet, feeling as if she were thrusting her way through a sea of hot syrup.

"No, it just looked that way." For some reason, Eizō took back his remark.

Haruyo suspected that her face probably *was* red because Eizō had denied what he'd seen.

"I told you a little about Okamura Masako before, didn't I? She was very happily married. A dependable, hard-working husband, beautiful children, a comfortable lifestyle. But she said an old flame had suddenly returned from the United States. Not just an ordinary 'old flame,' but the kind of man that any woman would find attractive. Perfect in every way. The consummate lover, too. But often she wouldn't hear from him for long stretches of time, as if he'd vanished into thin air. She felt sure that he was involved with lots of women, although she hadn't a shred of proof of that. But she could imagine him being perfectly satisfying to each and every one of those women. He's that type of man. At least that's how Masako described him." Haruyo's voice was shrill.

"What is it that you want to say, Haruyo? On a fine morning like this, that sort of talk just doesn't make sense." Eizō acted as if he wanted to devote himself to his planting, and yet he didn't reject Haruyo.

"Am I strange?" pressed Haruyo. If Eizō didn't think her strange, then there was something really the matter with *him*.

"No, I don't think you're strange," replied Eizō, after a moment of silence.

Haruyo scrutinized him, trying to decide whether or not he really meant that.

"Well, after Masako heard that the man had come back to Japan, she went into a tailspin. Things that had happened long ago came back to her as vividly as if they were occurring right then. That's what she said. The past burst into her present life and pulled the rug out from under her. I wonder if you can understand that feeling. We're both women, so I can understand it very well." Haruyo smiled slightly.

Eizō shook his head from side to side. Haruyo couldn't quite grasp the meaning of that gesture. Suddenly she felt as though a clear, slippery membrane, like gelatin, had formed between herself and Eizō.

"A long time ago, Okamura Masako invited me for a meal in a restaurant. At the time, I didn't know about those things at all. When I ran into her just the other day, she told me all about what had happened in the past. Anyway, we'd gone to quite a chic restaurant. While we were eating, that very man came in, accompanied by a woman. They mustn't have been used to going together to that restaurant. Because he's not the type of man to make such a blunder. One woman at one restaurant, another woman at another restaurant; he's skillful at keeping such things separate. So that time was a sheer coincidence. Anyway, Masako's face turned into a demon's, so I was stunned. I'll never forget that face. But at that point I still didn't know a thing. The delicious meal that Masako had been eating with relish got stuck in her throat. I wonder if you know how that feels. Food just won't go down your throat. It's that agonizing. It's not emotional pain, it's physical pain, it's organic pain . . . "

"Haruyo! Haruyo!" Eizō called her name to interrupt her story.

"No! You've got to hear me out. Because today, right now, I'm going to visit Okamura Masako."

"Right now?"

"Yes! She's in a terrible state."

"Weren't you going to take the children shopping this afternoon?"

"Are you serious? At a time like this?"

Haruyo was staring straight ahead of her. Eizō's face was about three feet away. Haruyo glared at that face as if it were a sworn enemy's.

Hasn't he seen the light yet? Haruyo wondered.

At the same time, she realized that she was deliberately destroying the secure life that she'd depended on so much. Behind Eizō many yellow tulips were blooming. They were lifting their heads that were growing hardier by the day. The bright morning sunshine was scattered like gold dust across the green lawn.

"Why do you suppose Okamura Masako loved a man who tormented her like that? It was because he loved her completely. As long as they were alone together, she was perfectly fulfilled. Her joy at those times and her anguish at other times were entwined, and they were binding her like a rope. A man who enthralls a woman— that's the sort of man Igawa Toshiaki was." Haruyo abruptly stopped speaking.

"That name sounds familiar," said Eizō, his face registering interest in what Haruyo had just said.

"As a matter of fact, he committed suicide. He jumped from a building. Even though he wasn't that type at all."

"What line of work was he in?"

"He worked at the Ministry of Foreign Affairs. He jumped off a building near there, enticed by a red balloon, apparently."

"Did you read this morning's newspaper?" Eizō didn't stop what he was doing, but his tone of voice seemed to change.

An element of Haruyo's tale and part of a true story corresponded, so Haruyo again scrutinized Eizō.

"That's why I have to rush to Masako's place immediately," she said, aware that she was saying something a bit different from earlier.

"Let's go. I'll go with you," said Eizō.

"What?" cried Haruyo, startled.

"I'll drive today. Because you're all worked up." Eizō stood motionless, holding the handle of the shovel with both hands.

Haruyo was dumbstruck. In her husband's considerate words, she sensed something closing in on her menacingly, like a sign painted in garish gold letters.

"Shouldn't you visit the family of the man who committed suicide?" said Eizō.

He was being his usual thoughtful self, but now his thoughtfulness had a peculiar ring. Haruyo felt as if the man standing in front of her had turned into a complete stranger.

"I didn't even know him. Why should I go? He's just a man who I saw once at that restaurant. He really was the kind of man that any woman would find attractive. It's impossible to define their appeal, but there are certain men who women are attracted to at a glance," said Haruyo earnestly.

"What was his name again?"

"Igawa Toshiaki."

"He has a good name, too."

"You'd never dream that a man like that would commit suicide. That's what Masako said," said Haruyo, realizing that her story was getting confused. Because since reading the article about the suicide, she couldn't have had a chance to talk to Okamura Masako.

"Oh, really. I see. Well, I'll pull the car out. You hurry and change your clothes. You have to rush, don't you? We'll go together to Okamura Masako's home," said Eizō casually.

"Dear!" Haruyo looked at Eizō. She gave him a hard stare, feeling as if he was treating her cruelly.

"You can relax. Because I'll drive," Eizō said coolly as he began walking toward the garage.

"Are you really going?" Haruyo cried.

"Yep, I really am," said Eizō, glancing back at her.

Strange Bonds

Yoshimura Ruriko went walking against the dusty wind. She'd reached an age when the pores of her skin were completely dried out, and she imagined that even if dust settled on her, it wouldn't cling to her. She was beginning to realize that what soils people is only the filth that comes out of them.

"I've grown more beautiful with age," Ruriko murmured.

Nearly every day she went walking like this. There were times when she walked to do errands, and other times, just for the sake of walking. She felt as if walking outdoors had become one of her body's involuntary functions. Probably another reason she walked so much was that she'd been healthy from when she was young. For a long, long time she'd been walking alone. Could you compare people's lives in terms of the total distance each person had walked in his lifetime? If so, she might well be in the top group. Men who'd gone to war were probably in a separate category. If she compared herself with men who'd gone to war, when she had been repatriated from Manchuria she'd walked a distance that would be unimaginable to the average woman. At that time, too, she was alone. Her husband and son had been drafted and sent to the front lines. A dry, grayish-green horizon stretched before her, a grayish-green wind was blowing, and a crimson evening sun was floating in midair. Droves of people were walking around her, but they were all refugees. Only the sun seemed as if it were truly alive.

She was in the bloom of youth when she'd witnessed that scene. She'd felt then as if her body were deeply stained with that crimson sun. But now, only a buoyant, dry body, to which even dust didn't cling, went moving along. Rays of yellowish sunlight streamed through the narrow spaces between buildings, but the sun itself was hidden. Yoshimura Ruriko went walking against the dusty wind typical of spring.

Behind her there was a thud. For a moment she thought that a lump of clay had been thrown against the sidewalk, and she turned around.

A man was lying there, face down. His body was eerily still. Its stillness was truly that of an object like a lump of clay. Ruriko approached him. When she'd taken five or six steps, she could look down at him from directly above. Blood was dripping from his face onto the pavement beneath it. Ruriko looked up. A seven- or eight-story building towered over her. An emergency staircase ran up the back of the building, and the door that opened onto the staircase landing at about the fifth floor was standing wide open. The back of the building faced an alley, so there were hardly any pedestrians around.

"Another suicide?" Ruriko murmured.

Those words plunged down through her body, echoing dryly.

Why did she keep finding herself at the scene of suicides? Ruriko's mind skimmed across her past.

A truck was parked at the back entrance of a building across the alley. Two workmen who were carrying a large carton toward that entrance interrupted their job to come rushing over. Several pedestrians approached from some distance away. Ruriko left the dead man in the care of those people and began walking again.

The man appeared to be meticulously groomed. His hair, too, which was a bit disheveled from his jump, was obviously well cared for. His face was utterly at odds with the overall impression he made. It had smashed on the pavement and turned into a pulpy mass of flesh.

Yoshimura Ruriko refrained from getting further involved in the situation, because the man seemed beyond a doubt to be dead. Until then, the people who had committed suicide that Ruriko had encountered were either completely healthy or not yet dead when she'd come upon them. In either case, Ruriko had talked with those people just before their deaths. But there was no longer any way to communicate with the man she'd just seen.

When she reached the subway station, the clock there read 4:48. Shortly before, Ruriko had come to the station by bus. Instead of immediately boarding the subway to return to the apartment complex where she lived, she'd decided to take a little stroll around the area, so she began walking. Her walk had no particular objective. It now seemed that because she'd inserted a slender interval between her periods of purposeful walking, she'd wound up encountering something that she otherwise would have been spared.

Suicide—that's right, thought Ruriko, *twice before I got involved with complete strangers who committed suicide.*

Her husband and son had died on the battlefield. Long before that, her younger sister, her only living relative at the time, had died. Over and over, death had occurred close at hand. As if that weren't enough, she encountered strangers who committed suicide.

Ruriko was pondering these things as she boarded the subway.

Today she'd gone to visit a woman friend who was in the hospital. When she got off the bus in front of XX Hospital, she saw cherry trees in full bloom all around the decrepit building. At that time, too, instead of immediately entering the hospital gate, she'd walked once completely around the wall surrounding the hospital. She'd never seen the area before. It took a full seven or eight minutes to get back to the gate. Large cherry trees stretched their limbs above the tall cinder block wall. In the gaps between the clusters of white blossoms, the darkly splotched walls of the hospital were visible. There were cherry trees by the wall, in the hospital courtyard, and in front of the entrance to the building.

"Don't you think it's strange? It's strange that cherry trees are blooming at a hospital. When you came here, didn't you think it was strange?" said Ruriko to Yasui Miyako. The two women had known each other since both were middle-aged, and for years they'd enjoyed a relationship that was friendly but not intimate.

"What's strange about it? It's you who say strange things. The cherry trees are blooming to cheer up the sick people. They say some philanthropist—I forget his name—donated those trees to the hospital. It was long ago, right after the end of the war, it seems. They've been here since then, so the cherry trees are old folks like us."

Miyako plopped down on the bed that was by the door in the four-patient room and prattled on.

"Well, that great do-gooder must have been a bit off his rocker, don't you think? Planting cherry trees at a hospital, of all the crazy things," Ruriko insisted as she sat down on a wooden stool.

"Everyone here loves them. No matter what you happen to think," Miyako retorted.

To an outsider, the two women might have appeared to be quarreling, but that was by no means so.

"The minute I got off the bus in front of here, it struck me. Just look at how lush those cherry blossoms are. They've really gone wild."

"What you're saying is that cherry blossoms and sick people don't go together."

"No, that's not it. They give me the creeps. It's as if the life of the sick people in the hospital had gone berserk and ended up like that.

As if the life force of the sick people had transformed itself into cherry blossoms. Cherry blossoms are vulgar. They're obscene. When all those cherry trees are in full bloom around the hospital wall, you can almost hear the shrieking and jabbering of the sick people coming out of the blossoms."

"There you go again with your foolish talk."

"A hospital should be cold and austere. It should be orderly, so as to prevent life from running rampant. Cold and strictly regimented. That's exactly why sick people can feel safe about entrusting themselves to it."

"Listen to her. A person who's never been hospitalized going on like that."

"It's indecent to plant cherry trees. When I see cherry trees blooming at a hospital like they are here today, this world of ours seems awfully vulgar."

"You're as young as ever. To say that sort of thing dead seriously. You know, Ruri?"

"Oh, 'Ruri,' is it?"

With that, the two women grinned at each other.

"The problem with names is that they don't grow old," said Ruriko, in a low-pitched voice that didn't match her girlish name.

"'Miyako' is the same way. Sounds like a schoolgirl," said Miyako, laughing gaily.

The three other women in the room joined in their mirth, their voices rising in faint ripples of near-laughter. All the patients in this room suffered from mild digestive disorders. Yasui Miyako was here because of chronic gastroenteritis, but her condition wasn't especially serious. She lived alone in a big house, so from last year she'd made it a habit to check herself into the hospital if she felt even slightly out of sorts. Ruriko drank the tea that Miyako had prepared for her, ate two rice crackers, chatted for a while, then left the room.

"You know the woman in the bed next to mine?" Miyako asked Ruriko as she accompanied her to the hospital entrance. "She's ten years younger than me but she doesn't look it, does she? Listen to what she told me. When she was young, she lived with her husband and his mother. I say 'she lived with her husband and his mother,' because the mother and her son had always lived together, just the two of them. And oh, was that mother crazy about her son! The young couple had their bedroom upstairs and the mother had hers downstairs, and in the middle of the night, the mother would rap on her ceiling with a broom handle. In other words, right beneath the bed of the young couple sleeping upstairs. Night after night that rapping would start up in the middle of the night. At that time, what sort of expression do you suppose the mother had on her face? 'Well, you can probably imagine,' says the woman in the bed next to mine. She never tells me what used to happen after that—the continuation of the story. She just tells me the same thing, over and over, I don't know how many times. Anyway, the other day the woman's son came to visit her here. When I saw how the two of them acted together, I understood everything in a wink. The story she tells me is actually her own story. She herself is in love with her only son, and every night in the middle of the night, she'd rap with a broom handle on the ceiling, around where her son and his wife were sleeping upstairs. And what sort of face would she be making? Well, you can imagine, can't you. I guess she was unable to stand the situation any longer, so she moved into this hospital. Because there isn't a single thing wrong with her. The woman is in love with her son. Of all the crazy things. But what's even crazier is her turning the story into a tale of her younger days and telling it as if she were the daughter-in-law. It's all the woman ever talks about."

Yasui Miyako blurted out the story without pausing for breath. She must have been bursting to tell it to Ruriko when they were back in the room.

"You see? It's no wonder cherries flourish like that at a hospital. How obscene can you get!" said Ruriko. Then she left.

She rode the subway for a while, then transferred to another subway line. As she stood in the car, holding onto a strap, she could clearly see her reflection in the darkened window. She'd lived with this face for a very long time, and for better or worse, during these past ten years she'd become able to confront it directly. When she was young, although others had thought her beautiful, she'd been plagued by self-loathing. But at some point that feeling had dropped away, like a clump of hair falling out, and she'd come to see herself as clear and unencumbered as a smooth bald pate.

She got off the subway, and after walking ten minutes, she reached her apartment complex. Then she walked for five or six minutes inside the complex. It was huge. Ruriko walked without paying much attention to her surroundings. She was even apt to forget what sorts of people were living in the same building as she.

"Ruriko, Ruriko," called a young voice.

Yoshimura Ruriko stopped and gazed ahead of her through the dusk. A dirty little girl with fine long hair was standing there.

"Oh, it's that little one," Ruriko murmured.

About a year ago, Ruriko had begun occasionally running into her. The child would be roaming around by herself, or else with a pack of mischievous boys, the only girl among them. Ruriko didn't know what building the girl lived in, and she'd never seen anyone who looked as if he might be a family member. The past two or three times that the girl had seen Ruriko, she'd greeted her as "Ruriko." Ruriko couldn't tell from the girl's tone of voice if she was being friendly or was taunting her. Generally, for a child to call an old woman by her first name suggested that her mind was a bit twisted. The last time, Ruriko had asked the girl how she knew her name. At first the child wouldn't reply, but when Ruriko pressed her, she said that she'd seen Ruriko's address in this apartment complex on a list of Bereaved Families of the War Dead. How had the girl happened to see such a thing? Was someone around the age of her mother's mother among the war bereaved? In today's cheerful world, that phrase itself had a hoary ring. It was a phrase that Ruriko herself only remembered when she went to collect her survivor's pension.

"What's your name? Why do you approach me?" Ruriko asked.

The girl romped around the twilight gloom like a filly. In the daylight she looked like a dirty urchin, but now, in the lamplight, her fine hair looked remarkably beautiful.

"I wonder why? I wonder why?" said the girl merrily. Again she frisked around, and then she galloped away on her long slender legs.

Ruriko tucked the girl's appearance away into a corner of her mind, climbed three flights of stairs, and pulled the knob of the door to her room. She was in the habit of leaving the door unlocked.

THE OCEAN WIND had been terribly cold that night. Rough waves were breaking, and the ship lurched from side to side. The sky had been overcast during the day, and that grayness seemed to have simply deepened into blackness. Neither moon nor stars was visible; there were only the rough waves, like countless sea monsters exhaling ferocious breath.

This scene wasn't the one she'd witnessed while riding the ferry from Pusan, Korea back to Japan right after the war ended, thirty years ago. But probably her memory of the more recent journey was mixed up with images from her voyage on the Japan Sea right after the war, because both times the ocean had been churned up by typhoonlike winds. The other journey had taken place on the Seto Inland Sea, where normally there are no rough waves. But that trip, too, had been over twenty years ago.

Ruriko saw a person's black shadow moving sluggishly across the deck, toward the ship's bow. A man wearing a jacket appeared. His entire body looked as lifeless as an object. That was eerily evident even in the dim light. The man made such a strange impression on her that Ruriko kept standing at the door leading to the deck, watching him from behind. She'd been standing there for nearly an hour, gazing at the turbulent ocean, and that image was superimposed on the man she was now watching. What Ruriko had been recalling as she stood there, during that time, in that place, was, after all, the rough sea that she'd gazed at from the deck of the ferry that she'd ridden from Pusan.

The man glanced back in her direction. He seemed to have seen Ruriko, who was leaning against the doorway. But immediately he again began walking toward the ship's bow. No one else was around. No one in the world would think of coming out on the deck to enjoy the ocean on a night such as this, in the dead of winter, when a gale was blowing with nearly the force of a typhoon.

Ruriko moved from the doorway out to the deck. The cold wind seemed about to knock her down. The man had his back to her. He was gripping the handrail at the bow with both hands and leaning forward, peering into the ocean. Again the man glanced behind him. This time it was clear that he saw Ruriko. For a moment he gave her a steely look; then he turned around again and leaned over to peer into the ocean. Finally, he threw one of his long legs over the guardrail, and keeping a tight grip on it, for the third time he glanced back at Ruriko.

"Won't you tell me not to do it?" said the man.

The remark made Ruriko realize that the man was about to commit suicide.

"Tell me, lady, tell me!" he urged, his voice rising.

The man was still young. He looked like a factory worker, maybe because of his jacket. It vaguely occurred to Ruriko that if he were a student, he probably wouldn't make an appeal to her like that.

Behind the man only an ink-black sea was visible. On both sides of the ship, waves were being tossed up. They were like starving seals, panting breathlessly as they awaited the flesh of the man who was about to jump.

"Why won't you tell me? I always thought women were more softhearted," said the man again.

Ruriko thought that perhaps the man had been disappointed in love. But throughout the encounter, she just stood there stiffly, in silence. She stared at the man, and then she stared at the rough ocean behind him. That ocean was superimposed on the ocean she'd seen from the deck of the ferry that she'd taken from Pusan.

The man jumped. Instantly, he was swallowed up by the black ocean.

Ruriko returned to her third-class cabin. Lying face up on her mat, she carried on an imaginary conversation with the man.

"Won't you tell me not to do it?" asked the man.

"Why must I try to change your fate?" said Ruriko.

"Tell me, lady, tell me," said the man.

"What on earth should I say? Should I say that being here is better than being over there? Should I offer a lot of proof to convince you that being here is better? I can't do that. For me, there would be nothing in this world as hard as that," said Ruriko.

"Why won't you tell me? I always thought women were more soft-hearted," said the man.

"All I can do for you is keep quiet. I don't have enough confidence to try to change another person's fate," said Ruriko.

As she lay face up in her third-class cabin, Ruriko had thought these things, but it wasn't that she felt she should have responded this way to the man. At the time, Ruriko had been forty-eight years old.

Then again, far across the years, in her mind she could see that rough sea she'd gazed at from the deck of the ferry that she'd taken from Pusan. It seemed far removed, and at the same time, she felt as if she were right there. That rough Japan Sea. On that winter night she'd stood on the deck, with the wind slicing through her like a large, cold blade and the chill turning her body into an icicle, and she'd just kept staring at the ocean. The ocean was a jet-black expanse. There were vague traces of light where the sky must have been, but the sky and the ocean were indistinguishable. The pale glimmer of the whitecaps pounding against the ship's sides was the only color in the scene. There would be a roar, and a wave's spray would be tossed up. Each time, Ruriko felt as if her life itself were being lashed by the spray. She was forty-one years old at the time.

When she was forty-eight, aboard the ship on the turbulent Seto Inland Sea, there was a definite reason she kept remembering the rough sea that she'd gazed at from the deck of the ferry she'd taken from Pusan when she was forty-one. It was her memory of a certain person. That person was several years older than Ruriko, and his name was Haoka Izō.

The port of Pusan had been in a state of chaos, and passengers to Japan ended up waiting there for one week, then two weeks, and finally three weeks before they were able to board the boat. Ruriko and the other passengers had awaited the day of departure crammed together in a crowded warehouse. Ruriko had sat with a man who earlier had been riding in the same train compartment as she. Since Ruriko had been traveling alone and so had the man, the two of them had probably been drawn to each other instinctively as conversation partners. The man's only baggage was one suitcase. Ruriko had one bundle of articles tied in a cloth and two suitcases. When a person got up to go to the toilet or to get something to eat or drink, he had to either carry his baggage with him, no matter how heavy it was, or ask someone he knew well to look after it. If he left it unattended, it was bound to be stolen. Moreover, the baggage that these refugees were carrying was all that was left of their possessions. One night a person had come for Ruriko's companion, telling him that someone on board had become critically ill. The man got up and went with that person. It then occurred to Ruriko that perhaps her companion was a doctor. Before leaving, the man had entrusted his single piece of luggage to Ruriko. Ruriko wrapped her arms around her baggage and the man's, pressing it all close to her body, and sat waiting on the concrete floor. The passengers, packed into the warehouse like cattle, were all exhausted and sleeping. There wasn't enough space for each person to lie down, so they were sitting with their heads thrust between their knees, sleeping uncomfortably. The man didn't return for a very long time. Even if a person wasn't tired, the bitter cold created a numbing sort of drowsiness. Ruriko drifted off to sleep, and she awakened when she sensed people stirring in the early morning. The baggage that the man had entrusted to her was gone. She thought perhaps the man had returned while she was asleep and had taken the suitcase with him. But when he came back around noon, she realized that it wasn't so.

"Ah!" The man gave a little animal-like cry. It sounded as if, for just a moment, he felt his innards constrict painfully. Then he became just like a clay doll, without feeling or sensation. A deep, deep silence emanated from him.

Ruriko then realized that she'd done something terrible, out of carelessness. Like everyone else, she was too exhausted to have the energy to concern herself with anyone else's welfare.

"I'm so sorry," Ruriko said. She felt as if she was dealing with something that couldn't be made right simply by saying "I'm sorry," and that even if she said it hundreds of times, it wouldn't begin to make up for what had happened. It seemed to her that all the man's anguish was condensed in that animal-like cry, "Ah!" that he'd just uttered.

But as Ruriko apologized repeatedly, the man gradually became strangely cheerful. That gloomy look on his face when he'd said "Ah!" vanished completely.

"It's all right," he said.

"'All right'? How can you say such a thing!?" said Ruriko in astonishment. This was an entirely different matter than if she'd lost a change purse that the man had asked her to keep for him. That much was amply clear to her from the man's voice and facial expression a few moments before.

"Because I didn't have anything, when it comes right down to it. It's fine," said the man. He turned his palms upward and stretched out his hands as if to emphasize that he had nothing.

The following day Ruriko had boarded the ferry, still bewildered as to why the man had become strangely lighthearted. What with the commotion on board the boat and her exhaustion during the trip, the incident receded to the back of her mind. While on board, she caught a glimpse of the man just once. But before getting on the boat she'd repeatedly asked him his name and address. The man had brushed aside her concern, but finally he wrote the information down on a scrap of paper for her.

Afterward, searching for the man became Ruriko's most vital task. She paid a call at the address that he had written down, but as she'd expected, he wasn't there. Apparently it hadn't been a false address, however, and luckily, she was told where he had moved.

Ruriko had continued to search for the man. Wherever she went, either she would be given the address of another place to which he'd moved, or else, although she was assured that the man was living there, no matter how many times she returned, he was never at home. Contrary to what she'd imagined at first, Ruriko began to think that the man couldn't be a doctor. If he were he would surely be settled in one place. Someone had come to get the man, saying something about a person who was critically ill. What in the world could the man's occupation be? Ruriko wondered. Then after a while, she completely lost track of the man's whereabouts.

"Because I didn't have anything, when it comes right down to it. It's fine."

Ruriko gradually came to feel the man's words, spoken after he'd become strangely lighthearted, begin to live inside her.

"I didn't have anything, when it comes right down to it. It's fine."

Ruriko had actually said this a few times to Yasui Miyako. People and things—everything—had been wrenched from her, as if by centrifugal force, and had vanished somewhere.

RURIKO RECALLED THAT the second suicide scene she'd had the misfortune to encounter had taken place about ten years earlier. At that time, too, she'd been walking alone. It had been relatively recently, so she was no longer wandering around searching for Haoka Izō. But in her memory, for some reason the image of herself walking alone was superimposed on that of herself walking around in search of Haoka Izō.

When she looked back over her life, the pattern of her walking reminded her of the network of blood vessels that one sees in models of human anatomy. An ordinary woman probably follows a single, gently curving path, but Ruriko had zigzagged greatly in her wanderings.

Why had she walked around searching so single-mindedly for Haoka Izō? Certainly she'd wanted to apologize. But she also realized that just meeting him wouldn't mean that she had adequately apologized to him. Ruriko could never forget Haoka's voice and face at the moment he had cried "Ah!" and his face had contorted in anguish. At the same time, she could never forget how odd it seemed when, right after that, Haoka had suddenly become strangely lighthearted. Perhaps she'd wanted to ask him something, rather than to apologize. She'd been unable to clearly formulate what she wanted to ask, but little by little she'd felt the gist of her question becoming enmeshed with her life. That irrational question had slowly penetrated deep into her life.

About ten years before, Ruriko had been walking through a large new housing project. A small child had come out of a house with cream-colored mortar walls. Ruriko had sensed something unnatural about him, and she had stopped. The child was swerving like a sleepwalker.

"What's wrong, little boy?" Ruriko called out to the child.

"Aah, aah," the boy moaned lethargically.

Most of the homes in the complex had been completed. They were all alike, featuring the latest colors, shapes, and decorations; they looked like rows of dollhouses lined up side by side. Ruriko had been walking along thinking that the homes were like dollhouses when she saw the boy. Houses modeled on children's storybook fantasies that adults went along with. No, not quite, she thought. Houses modeled on the sugary dreams spun by children and women to which men forced themselves to adapt. Because children and women yearned so fiercely for the dreamlands found only in picture books, those dreamlands sprang out of their picture books and foisted themselves on a new housing complex. Even though picture-book dreams should never leave the pages of picture books, children and women transformed them into houses and defiled the dreams. Ruriko was walking around, absorbed in such random reflections.

The house that the boy had come out of was exactly the same type of dollhouse as the others, but something peculiar had erupted in it, like mold. Ruriko had sensed that because the boy had come out walking strangely and moaning something.

"Won't you tell me what's wrong, sonny?" Ruriko asked again.

The boy, who was four or five years old, raised his drowsy eyes and pointed inside the house. That gesture, too, was terribly lethargic.

Ruriko took two or three steps in the direction of the door that the boy had left open when he came out. There was a faint smell of gas. She stepped into the entryway. She didn't rush in. She had long ago lost the ability to be surprised by anything. She couldn't say just when she had lost that ability, even if she retraced her past.

A man was lying face up in the kitchen; gas filled the room. Ruriko shut off the gas and opened the window.

The man wasn't dead. But he wasn't really alive, either. He raised his vacant eyes and looked at Ruriko. That was the only sign that he was alive; his skin was already as cold as a corpse. Near him lay a scrap of paper, with just one line written with a felt marking pen.

"Whoever finds me, please let me die," Ruriko read out loud.

She looked at the man and saw that his eyes seemed to be saying those words. But he was almost dead. A vestige of his life was hovering between this world and the next world. Ruriko guessed that the man was in his late thirties.

"Can you hear me?" asked Ruriko. She felt as though she had nothing else to say besides that.

Although he wasn't uttering a sound or shedding tears, somewhere inside his immobile body the man seemed to be sobbing. He was lamenting not his imminent death, but having been alive. Somehow, Ruriko sensed that.

"Can you see?" asked Ruriko. In contrast to when she was riding on the ship on the Japan Inland Sea, this time it was only Ruriko who was talking.

A kitchen with smart, flower-patterned wallpaper; pink curtains; a shiny, stainless-steel sink; multicolored dishes; a birdcage without a bird; and a red-checked apron that evidently belonged to the man's wife. It was as if the man had been destroyed by the sentimental dreamland that had been frantically, insistently created by his children and wife inside this home that seemed to come straight from the pages of a picture book. Because this house and the dying man were utterly alien to each other.

Ruriko gazed at the man one last time, confirmed in his eyes the words "Whoever finds me, please let me die," then left the house.

"Sonny, who is that man?" Ruriko asked the boy, who was standing in the sunlight in the garden.

"It's Papa. He's sleeping, really well."

The child's response was unexpectedly clear. Shortly before, he'd apparently been in a fog from having inhaled some gas.

"He's sleeping?"

"Papa just won't get up. I pounded and kicked him and he opened his eyes."

"Really? When?"

"A little while ago."

"Where were you before, sonny?"

"With Mama."

"Where's Mama?"

"She's talking in that house over there." The boy pointed to a house some distance away.

"When was this?"

"Noon."

"It's already three o'clock."

"When I went home Papa was sleeping. I pounded and kicked him, and he opened his eyes."

"Really? And then what?"

"He told me, 'Turn on the gas.'"

"Oh, my! But why didn't Papa do that?"

"He said he was too sleepy to get up. When I turned on the gas, Papa said, 'Thank you,' and he fell fast asleep."

Since the boy had inhaled the fresh air he seemed to have returned to normal; he spoke falteringly, but he answered everything. Ruriko pictured the boy turning on the gas as he was asked to do by his father, who hadn't taken quite enough sleeping pills to die. Then the boy had probably continued to play innocently, scampering back and forth between his house and the yard. During those three hours his father must have inhaled plenty of gas.

Ruriko stood silently with the boy in the sunny garden. She didn't know what else to do. Because the man had written, "Whoever finds me, please let me die."

The scene that followed was a predictable one. The wife returned, wearing sugar-sweet clothes and makeup; then a great commotion ensued. The neighbors came rushing over. The man was already dead and the wife wept hysterically. But Ruriko kept listening intently not to that voice, but to the sobbing she'd heard inside the man a little while ago, just before he had died. She'd been listening to the man's true self, who had been forced to say, "I've had enough of this life." A wan halo had seemed to surround the man's sobbing, because a little child had been his accomplice.

Then Ruriko suddenly recalled another death. That man in the housing project had actively pursued death, but in the other case, death had assaulted a woman like a rapist.

When Ruriko was twenty-seven years old, she'd had a twenty-three-year-old sister who was her only sibling. Her sister was newly married and full of life. One day she phoned the home of Ruriko's next-door neighbor and asked to speak to Ruriko. She said her stomach hurt and asked Ruriko to come right away. Ruriko's sister was borrowing someone else's phone too. It was back in the days when the ordinary household didn't have a telephone. Ruriko took a train and went. When she arrived, her sister was in bed, thrashing in agony. Between gasps, she told Ruriko that from two days before she'd had a dull pain in her lower abdomen, as if it was full of stones, but that day, while eating lunch, she was suddenly wracked with acute pain. She'd called for a doctor, but he hadn't arrived yet. At the end of the day the doctor came and diagnosed her condition as an ectopic pregnancy. It was too late to operate. Because of the great amount of internal hemorrhaging her blood pressure was very low, so she couldn't have anesthesia. If the doctor were to take a chance and perform surgery, he would probably have to operate without anesthesia. Ruriko's sister's husband came home from work to help the doctor and Ruriko care for his wife. Her sister died, writhing in pain so excruciating that even those three adults couldn't hold her down. Not quite seven hours had passed since Ruriko had received the phone call. Ruriko had witnessed, in that brief interval, the end of a human life. Her sister's writhing body had appeared to be crying out desperately, "I want to live!" At the same time it seemed to be saying, "I've had enough of this life!"

Ruriko recalled another time, many years before her sister's death, when Ruriko had still been in elementary school. She'd been forced to witness, from start to finish, the protracted death of an elderly female relative who lived with her family. The woman wasn't ill, but she was demented. Numerous people—relatives, friends, and family members—took turns crowding around the dying woman's bed to peer at her. Although it seemed as if the end was imminent, she simply would not die but lingered for one more day, then another. Her heart was stubborn, and it seemed as if it would detain the old woman in this world forever. But everything else in her body besides her heart was totally debilitated, so she couldn't even say a word. Still, her heart kept beating, as if out of spite, and the old woman just could not die. The crowds of people who gathered around her bed insisted on showering her with farewell words and encouragement and reminiscences that she no longer had any desire to hear. Ruriko, although still a child, had thought that to be surrounded by well-wishers like that, up until the moment of death, must be torture. Death had held off for one week, then for another week. During that time the old lady, who seemed to harbor the heart of a fox or badger, had had to keep battling against that robust part of herself.

A human being is like a haunted house, thought Ruriko, as she glanced back again and again across her past. But her thoughts would trail off and disappear.

RURIKO LEFT HER APARTMENT in the housing complex, because that girl whom she often encountered came to get her.

"Hey there, come and have a look," said the girl, and bounded down the stairs ahead of Ruriko. On the surface she just looked unkempt, but she had a bit of the sexiness of a juvenile delinquent about her.

"What is it?" asked Ruriko, as she followed the girl quickly through the early afternoon sunlight. She wasn't especially interested in the child, but she wanted to understand why she was always coming after her.

The girl walked briskly five or six steps ahead of Ruriko on the sidewalk that ran through the huge apartment complex. The last time that Ruriko had run into the girl was on her way home from visiting Yasui Miyako in the hospital. About a month had passed since then. Probably the branches of the cherry trees at the hospital were now covered with young leaves. It suddenly occurred to Ruriko to go straight from here to visit Yasui Miyako, since she hadn't seen her in quite a while.

"Looooky, looooky," cried the girl, like an owl.

Right ahead of them in the complex was a row of single-family homes. Black smoke was rising in the garden of one of them. Ruriko knew the house well, because its summer orange tree, luxuriant with glossy leaves and large yellow fruit, was impressive. But now that summer orange tree was on fire. A woman of thirty-four or thirty-five, probably the woman of that house, was staring up at it in stupefaction.

"What in the world . . ?" said Ruriko to the girl.

"Loony," said the girl and squealed with laughter.

"That woman?"

"They say she cracked up the day before yesterday. That she poured oil over that tree she's been tending so carefully and set it on fire."

"It's true," murmured Ruriko; then she glanced around the area. In a huge residential complex like this, it was no wonder if at least one person with the normal amount of desire went mad. That big new housing complex where she'd witnessed the suicide had been like that too. She'd sensed something like the fever of madness in all those women vying to create the sweetest sugar-candy cottage. Of course, Ruriko had no way of knowing why this woman in front of her had gone mad.

"To burn a living tree is dreadful . . . a tree that's still alive," said Ruriko to the girl, but it wasn't likely that the child could understand what she meant.

The area was permeated with the scorched, sweet-sour stench of the oil-drenched summer orange tree. The woman's vacant eyes were stretched wide open, and she was staring at the tree that was blazing and sending up black smoke. Each round yellow orange looked to Ruriko like a baby. It seemed as if they were being burned to death.

The woman's derangement might be related to a baby. Then again, it might not, but Ruriko had begun to feel that way.

"Wild, isn't it? Well, see you later," said the girl, and she began to run off.

"Why do you seek me out?" Ruriko asked, determined to pry an answer out of the girl today.

"I wonder why, I wonder why." The girl rolled her round eyes.

"What's your name?"

"My name? It's Yoshimura Ruriko."

"Shame on you, teasing an old woman."

As if she'd been sent flying by Ruriko's tone of rebuke, the girl bounded away down the sidewalk. Ruriko watched her departing figure from behind. A boy of around the same age as the girl was coming toward her, and when he and the girl passed each other, both of them reached out, pretending to grab the other one. Ruriko walked over to the boy and asked, "That girl, what's her name?"

"Yoshimura Ruriko," replied the boy curtly, then he continued on his way.

Unable to tell whether or not he was teasing her too, Ruriko headed for the gate of the complex.

Far ahead of her, Ruriko could still see the girl's running figure. She felt as if the girl were bounding through her own past. As the girl's figure vanished into the distance, Ruriko paused momentarily, savoring the sensation that she had entered the twilight before she was born.

Ruriko left the huge apartment complex where the inferno of human life was contained within hundreds of reinforced concrete buildings. Then she boarded the subway and rode to the center of the city. From there she took a bus. Yasui Miyako was the perfect partner for a casual conversation.

Ruriko got off the bus in front of the hospital and looked up to see the luxuriant young leaves of the cherry trees covering the white walls. After entering the hospital, she felt like strolling around before going to Yasui Miyako's room. Here, too, was a place where each room harbored a living hell, but it wasn't as bad as the apartment complex. It seemed as if it should be the opposite, but it wasn't. Ruriko walked down the corridor absorbed in that thought.

"Take this to Mr. Haoka on the third floor. You know, the old man who doesn't say a word."

That voice caught Ruriko's attention.

Haoka. Haoka Izō.

Ruriko turned in the direction of the voice to see one nurse handing another one a packet of medicine.

Inside Ruriko, a spring went *boing*.

She couldn't actually call the man a close friend, but because she'd wandered in search of him for so long, she had gradually become intimate with him.

"If it's him, we have a strange bond," murmured Ruriko.

Whether "Haoka" was *that* Haoka, she didn't know. In any case, she decided to go up to the third floor, so she took the elevator. But she didn't see any such nameplate on the third floor of the old building where Miyako was, so she headed for the new building. Invalids wearing nightgowns that looked saturated with perspiration were walking around amid the inorganic background scenery— the soothing, cream-colored smooth walls and floors, the soft white acoustic ceilings. The scent of their tepid souls, mingled with their body odor, seemed to drift from the slovenly openings at the breast and skirt of their nightgowns.

Suddenly Ruriko stood stock-still. She'd been walking along the third-floor corridor looking at the nameplates posted beside each room door, and now, right before her eyes was the nameplate HAOKA IZŌ.

Thirty years ago, in the port of Pusan. Forced to wait for the boat's departure one week, two weeks, then three weeks. Stuck inside the warehouse used as a waiting room that was pervaded by the exhaustion of the dark swarm of people herded together there. The unwashed masses of people with no room to lie down, squatting and waiting for the boat's departure inside that cavernous warehouse, anger and anxiety and hope and fear mingling with their foul body odor. Everyone stretching their bloodshot eyes wide open, having slept fitfully or not at all. Everyone clutching the baggage containing their worldly possessions pared down to a bare minimum, the things they cherished more than life itself. It was then.

"Where are you going back to? Where in Japan?" Ruriko had asked earnestly.

"Where? Oh, nowhere in particular," the man had said.

The words "nowhere in particular" went well with his expression, which had grown strangely bright and seemed to be floating in midair.

"But please at least tell me where I can contact you," Ruriko had persisted.

The man must surely have lost his most precious possession. Otherwise, how could he have suddenly become so detached?

"A strange bond," murmured Ruriko, as she stood in front of the nameplate.

She thought that she'd buy some flowers at the shop on the first floor and then go visit him, so she walked away from the entrance to the room.

Ruriko had wanted to know what Haoka Izō had lost at that time. Perhaps that was why she'd wandered in search of him for so long. It had occurred to her that perhaps the suitcase contained the mortal remains of the person dearest to him. Or at least some such thing to which one would be extremely attached. . . . That was it, attachment. The longer Ruriko had wandered around searching in vain for Haoka, the more immense what he'd lost had come to seem to her. In her imagination, it had expanded to fill the whole world. But Haoka had said, "It doesn't matter."

Ruriko stood in front of the florist wondering which flowers to buy. It dawned on her that the flowers should be the color of atonement. Then she was startled at herself for suddenly having the peculiar notion of atonement. The flowers weren't for Haoka.

"Ruriko, what are you doing?" a voice said. Ruriko looked around to see Yasui Miyako standing there in her hospital gown.

"Oh, I was just mulling something over," said Ruriko, realizing that she couldn't articulate what she'd just been thinking.

"Listen to this creepy story, will you?" Miyako said as she started to walk.

"About where and who?" Ruriko asked. She too began walking, but her mind was elsewhere.

"A story about someone who ate a chicken," said Miyako in a hoarse voice. Although the weather was warm, she seemed to have a slight cold.

"There's nothing odd about that, is there? Everybody eats chicken," Ruriko said bluntly. She was beginning to feel that she probably wouldn't visit Haoka's room.

"Just listen, will you? It's a creepy story, I'm sure you'll agree." Miyako was seized by a terrible coughing fit.

As Ruriko stood beside her, waiting for that to be over, she shifted her attention away from Haoka and let her thoughts run far, far into her past. Again she seemed to see the girl called Yoshimura Ruriko sprinting, as if on stepping-stones, across the days of Ruriko's own past that stretched into infinity, and entering the twilight before she was born.

Unless it were possible to live one's life in reverse, undoing everything that one had done, there was no way to atone for the life one had lived. For some reason, Ruriko had begun to feel that way.

When Miyako stopped coughing, she told her tale without pausing for breath.

"It's about that woman in the bed next to mine. You know, the one who's in love with her son. She said that long ago, during the war, she was keeping a chicken at her house. It was a hen—she'd named it Hanako—and oh, how she doted on that chicken, she said. Anyway, it was during the war, so it wasn't an age when people were keeping dogs and cats as pets; at most, they might have had a chicken. The woman's such a softy. She was always burbling, 'Miss Hanako, Miss Hanako,' and making a big fuss over it. That hen was her reason for living. Well, do you begin to see the connection? This was when the woman was still young, way before the son she's in love with was born. In general, her affectionate nature makes her capable of things that are normally unthinkable, like coddling a hen that way and being in love with your own son. So to get back to the story, the woman ate that very chicken."

"What!?" said Ruriko, jolted back to reality.

"Hanako gradually deteriorated until she was no longer her old self. It was right after Japan lost the war, when there wasn't any food, so the woman decided to just go ahead and eat Hanako."

"Did she kill the hen herself?" Ruriko felt her interest piqued when she pictured the gory details.

"I wouldn't know about that. That's another subject; the point is that she ate her. Ordinarily, if you keep chickens it's only natural to eat them. But to eat a chicken that you'd loved like a human, that's a different matter, isn't it?"

"Did the woman tell the story that way?" Ruriko asked half-heartedly.

"No, I'm giving you my version. It's as if she ate human flesh. Don't you think so? I felt sure you'd say that."

"Well, you have a point."

"What a lame reaction!"

"You go back to your room first. I'll be there soon," said Ruriko, thinking that she'd visit Haoka Izō's room after all. She went downstairs again, in order to go to the florist she'd seen there.

Flowers the color of atonement, she thought. There were some long-stemmed, pure white flowers. They were hothouse flowers called calla lilies, the florist said. They were expensive, but Ruriko bought three of them. She hadn't held flowers in her hands for decades. She elevated them a bit and began walking down the corridor in the direction of the new building. She'd intended the white bouquet for Haoka Izō, but she felt, instead, that she was raising it in homage to her long, long past, which her mind had skimmed across a while before.

Just then Ruriko realized that an ambulance had arrived at the hospital's front entrance, its siren blaring. She stopped and looked back. People were rushing in that direction in alarm, and voices were gathering there. Within moments, a stretcher carried by two nurses came weaving toward the spot where Ruriko was standing.

"What is it? What happened?"

"Evidently a traffic accident."

"Loads of glass slivers were sticking out of both her hands."

"Did you actually see it?"

"When the windshield shatters, glass flies everywhere—not just into the person's hands, but even into their eyes."

"Was that person driving?"

"Is it a man or a woman?"

"I don't know."

"What? You don't even know that?!"

The stretcher, covered entirely with a white drape, passed through people's conversations and in front of Ruriko. As Ruriko followed it with her eyes, she noticed that there was a difference in levels between the old and new buildings. When she was crossing between the two, one of the nurses tried to raise the stretcher up and she lost her balance and stumbled, so the stretcher tilted sharply. A navy blue purse slid out from beneath the white drape and its contents spilled out.

"Oh, pick those things up, will you, ma'am?" The other nurse happened to catch Ruriko's eye, and she said that as if issuing an order. The two nurses hurried on with the stretcher, as though they'd entrusted the task to her.

Ruriko moved up a few steps and picked up makeup and a wallet. When she was putting these into the purse, she noticed inside a piece of stationery folded in quarters with the words "suicide note" written on it.

"Here we go again," she murmured.

Then she followed the stretcher. If she were to place the purse on it, it would probably fall off again. So, as if she were the relative or friend of the person beneath that white drape, she quietly walked along, holding the purse. Judging from the careful way the nurses were carrying the stretcher, the person mustn't have been dead. It seemed fitting to Ruriko to set the white flowers that she was holding there, so she placed them gently near the person's feet. The three large white flowers jiggled gently from side to side, in accordance with the hasty or slow pace at which the nurses carried the stretcher.

"Suicide note."

The words were branded in her mind's eye.

One after another, they go on dying.

Long ago, her only living relative, her younger sister, had died. During the war countless people had died, her husband and son among them. Then after the war, so many people had died of starvation or disease. On top of all that, oddly enough, strangers committed suicide and died right in front of her.

Strange bonds, mused Ruriko.

The stretcher entered the waiting room adjoining the operating room and was stopped.

"There's a suicide note inside," said Ruriko, handing the purse to one of the nurses. She'd meant to say, "There's something important inside."

The nurse gingerly opened the handbag and peeked inside it. Then she said to the other nurse, "Yamakawa Sakiko. The character for 'saki,' that means 'to bloom.' 'Along a mountain stream, flowers bloom.' A nice name, isn't it."

The operating room door opened from inside. Another nurse and a doctor came out, and they carried the stretcher into the room. The door was closed and the person beneath the white drape disappeared from Ruriko's sight. The flowers went inside too.

"I wonder if they'll operate on her in that condition."

"They're going to see whether or not they can."

The two nurses who had carried the stretcher from the front entrance were whispering together.

Ruriko stood at the threshold between the waiting room and the corridor, reluctant to leave.

"What sort of person is she?" Ruriko simply asked.

The nurse holding the purse closed it securely, then tossed it onto a chair in the waiting room.

"A young woman. Around my age." The plump-lipped young nurse smiled sweetly.

"I didn't have anything, when it comes right down to it. It's fine." Ruriko thought that perhaps that was what the note said. Or rather, for a moment she imagined secretly replacing the contents of the suicide note with those words. So if the woman woke up, she could see it. But she would probably wake up in the other world and have to see it from there. Even so, that would surely be a glorious awakening.

Along a mountain stream, flowers bloom. The flowers that Ruriko had just bought, flowers the color of atonement, passed through the operating room, entered an empty car, and receded through space. Far, far away in space, along a mountain stream in a misty land, the same pure white flowers are flourishing. In perfect silence, they are thriving.

S ELECTED B IBLIOGRAPHY

(Unless otherwise noted, the place of publication of all Japanese-language works is Tokyo.)

W ORKS BY T AKAHASHI T AKAKO IN J APANESE

Work Compiled by the Author

Takahashi Takako jisen shōsetsushū (Takahashi Takako's self-selected literary works). 4 vols. Kōdansha, 1994. (Includes five novels, eleven short stories, one novella [*The House of Rebirth*], four new essays, and the linked short story collection *Lonely Woman*.)

Novels

(*Denotes novel not included in Takahashi Takako jisen shōsetsushū*)*

*Sora no hate made (To the end of the sky). Shinchōsha, 1973.

Botsuraku fūkei (A ruined landscape). Kawade Shobō Shinsha, 1974.
Yūwakusha (The tempter). Kōdansha, 1976.
Ten no mizuumi (The heavenly lake). Shinchōsha, 1977.
Arano (Wasteland). Kawade Shobō Shinsha, 1980.
Yosooi seyo, waga tamashii yo (Prepare thyself, my soul). Shinchōsha, 1982.
Ikari no ko (Child of wrath). Kōdansha, 1985.
Bōmeisha (Exile). Kōdansha, 1995.
Kimi no naka no mishiranu onna (The unknown woman within you).
    Kōdansha, 2001.
Kirei na hito (A beautiful person). Kōdansha, 2003.

Linked Short-Story Collection

Ronrii ūman (Lonely woman). Shūeisha, 1977.

Short Story and Novella Collections

Kanata no mizu oto (Yonder sound of water). Kōdansha, 1971.
Hone no shiro (Castle of bones). Kyoto: Jimbun Shoin, 1972.
Sōmen (Double mask). Kawade Shobō Shinsha, 1972.
Kyōsei kūkan (Symbiotic space). Shinchōsha, 1973.
Ushinawareta e (The lost picture). Kawade Shobō Shinsha, 1974.
Hanayagu hi (The glorious day). Kōdansha, 1975.
Ningyō ai (Doll love). Kōdansha, 1978.
Ayashimi (Suspicion). Shinchōsha, 1981.
Tōku, kutsū no tani o aruite iru toki (As I walk through the endless val-
    ley of woe). Kōdansha, 1983.

Collected Essays

Tamashii no inu (Soul dogs). Kōdansha, 1975.
Kioku no kurasa (The darkness of memory). Kyoto: Jimbun Shoin, 1977.
Odoroita hana (Startled flowers). Kyoto: Jimbun Shoin, 1980.
Sakai ni ite (On the border). Kōdansha, 1995.
Hōsha suru omoi (Reflections that radiate). Kōdansha, 1997.
Kono bannen to iu toki (These twilight years). Kōdansha, 2002.

Memoirs

Takahashi Kazumi no omoide (Memories of Takahashi Kazumi). Kōsōsha, 1977.

Takahashi Kazumi to iu hito: nijūgo-nen no ato ni (Remembering Takahashi Kazumi: Twenty-five years later). Kawade Shobō Shinsha, 1997.

Watashi no tōtta michi (The path I traveled). Kōdansha, 1999.

Spiritual Writings

Reiteki na shuppatsu (Spiritual departure). Joshi Pauro Kai, 1985.

Kami no tobihi (Divine sparks). Joshi Pauro Kai, 1986.

Mizu soshite honō (Water and fire). Joshi Pauro Kai, 1989.

Tochi no chikara (The power of place). Joshi Pauro Kai, 1992.

"Uchinaru shiro" ni tsuite omou koto (Reflections on the "interior castle"). Self-published, 1992.

Hajimari e (Toward the origin). Joshi Pauro Kai, 1993.

Published Dialogues and Roundtable Discussions

Endō Shūsaku and Takahashi Takako. "Sukui to bungaku to" (Salvation and literature). *Fujin Kōron* 63 (2) (February 1978): 196–203.

Tsushima Yūko and Takahashi Takako. "Onna no sei to otoko no me" (Female sexuality and the male gaze). *Waseda Bungaku* 30 (November 1978): 4–14.

Ōba Minako and Takahashi Takako. *Taidan: sei to shite no onna* (A dialogue on woman as a sexual being). Kōdansha, 1979.

Kawamura Jirō, Takahashi Takako, and Tsushima Yūko. "Joryū o tsukiugokasu mono" (What compels women writers). *Kokubungaku Kaishaku to Kyōzai no Kenkyū* 25 (15) (December 1980): 6–25.

Ōba Minako and Takahashi Takako. "Ikitsuzukeru to iu koto—sonzai · shūkyō · hyōgen" (To keep on living: Life, religion, expression)." *Gunzō* 36 (9) (September 1981): 234–55.

Ōba Minako and Takahashi Takako. "Kongenteki na seimei no fukashigi" (The fundamental mystery of life). *Shinchō* 79 (12) (December 1982): 170–200.

Haniya Yutaka and Takahashi Takako. "Tamashii no katsubō: ōfuku shokan to taiwa" (The soul's thirst: Correspondence and conversation). *Gunzō* 49 (1) (January 1994): 290–335.

Takahashi Takako. *Ishiki to sonzai no nazo: aru shūkyōsha to no taiwa* (The enigma of consciousness and existence: A dialogue with a clergyperson). Kōdansha, 1996.

WORKS BY TAKAHASHI TAKAKO IN ENGLISH

"Congruent Figures." Trans. of "Sōjikei." Trans. Noriko Mizuta Lippit. In *Stories by Contemporary Japanese Women Writers,* trans. and ed. Noriko Mizuta Lippit and Kyoko Iriye Selden. Armonk, N.Y.: M.E. Sharpe, 1982, 153–81. Reprinted in *Japanese Women Writers: Twentieth-Century Short Fiction,* trans. and ed. Noriko Mizuta Lippit and Kyoko Iriye Selden. Armonk, N.Y.: M. E. Sharpe, 1991, 168–93.

"Doll Love." Trans. of "Ningyō ai." Trans. Mona Nagai and Yukiko Tanaka. In *This Kind of Woman: Ten Stories by Japanese Women Writers, 1960–1976,* ed. Yukiko Tanaka and Elizabeth Hanson. Stanford: Stanford University Press, 1982, 197–223.

"The Oracle." Trans. of "Otsuge." Trans. Nina Blake. *Review of Japanese Culture and Society* 3 (1) (December 1989): 97–110.

"Invalid." Trans. of "Byōshin." Trans. Van C. Gessel. *Mānoa: A Pacific Journal of International Writing* 3 (2) (Fall 1991): 132–40.

CRITICISM ON TAKAHASHI TAKAKO'S LITERATURE

In Japanese

Ueda Miyoji, Kawamura Jirō, and Hiraoka Tokuyoshi. "Joryū sakka no shinkeikō (zadankai)" (New trends in women's writing [Round-table discussion]). *Gunzō* 30 (3) (March 1975): 144–69.

Kōno Taeko, Saeki Shōichi, and Mori Atsushi. "Dokusho teidan: Takahashi Takako, *Ronrii ūman*" (A tripartite discussion on Takahashi Takako's *Lonely Woman*). *Bungei* 16 (10) (October 1977): 270–80.

Yoshikawa Toyoko. "Takahashi Takako—fukashi no 'josei' no kyūzaisha" (Takahashi Takako: Savior of an invisible 'woman'). *Kokubungaku Kaishaku to Kanshō* 44 (4) (April 1979): 159–66.

Irie Takanori. "Aku no hate e no tabi—Takahashi Takako ron" (Journey to the extremity of evil: On Takahashi Takako). *Shinchō* 78 (4) (April 1981): 146–70.

Matsumoto Tōru. "Kaisetsu" (Commentary). In *Ronrii ūman* (Lonely woman). Shūeisha, 1982, 209–17.

Odagiri Hiroko. "Kawaki o mitasu mono—Takahashi Takako no sekai" (What quenches thirst: The world of Takahashi Takako). In *Nihon katorishizumu to bungaku—Inoue Yōji · Endō Shūsaku · Takahashi Takako* (Japanese Catholicism: Inoue Yōji, Endō Shūsaku, and Takahashi Takako), ed. Toda Yoshio. Taimeidō, 1982, 129–68. (Also see 186–91.)

Hirai Nori. "Takahashi Takako ron—'aku' no kōzō" (On Takahashi Takako: The structure of 'evil'). *Gakuen* 530 (February 1984): 48–60.

Saegusa Kazuko. *Sayonara otoko no jidai* (Farewell to the era of men). Kyoto: Jimbun Shoin, 1984, passim.

Yamauchi Yukito. "Ikirareta jiga—Takahashi Takako ron" (The self that was able to survive: On Takahashi Takako). *Gunzō* 39 (6) (June 1984): 87–106.

——. "'Akui' no bungaku—Takahashi Takako *Yūwakusha* made" (Literature of malice: Takahashi Takako's fiction through *The Tempter*). *Gunzō* 39 (11) (November 1984): 188–202.

——. "'Kami' no bungaku—Takahashi Takako *Yūwakusha* igo" (Divinely inspired literature: Takahashi Takako's fiction since *The Tempter*). *Gunzō* 40 (9) (September 1985): 197–216.

Yonaha Keiko. "Takahashi Takako ron" (On Takahashi Takako). In *Gendai joryū sakka ron* (On contemporary Japanese women writers). Shimbisha, 1986, 30–63.

Kazusa Hideo. "Takahashi Takako ron" (On Takahashi Takako). In *Uchinaru kiseki—nana-nin no sakkatachi* (Inner traces: Seven authors). Chōbunsha, 1990, 105–55.

Sunami Toshiko. *Takahashi Takako ron* (On Takahashi Takako). Ōfūsha, 1992.

Hasegawa Kei. "Kodokusha aruiwa itsudatsusha no kyōki—Takahashi Takako *Ronrii ūman* o chūshin ni" (The madness of the lonely or the deviant: Centering on Takahashi Takako's *Lonely Woman*). *Shin Nihon Bungaku* 48 (10) (October 1993): 60–65.

Nakagawa Shigemi. "Seimei no fūkei—Takahashi Takako to 'inochi'" (A dynamic landscape: Takahashi Takako and 'vitality'). *Speakable memories katarikakeru kioku: bungaku to jendā sutadīzu* (Speakable memories: Literature and gender studies). Ozawa Shoten, 1999, 97–113.

Nakagawa Shigemi and Hasegawa Kei, eds. *Takahashi Takako no fūkei* (Takahashi Takako's literary landscape). Sairyūsha, 1999.

In English

Monnet, Livia. "'Child of Wrath': The Literature of Takahashi Takako." *The Transactions of the Asiatic Society of Japan*, fourth series, vol. 5 (1990): 87–121.

Mori, Maryellen T. "The Subversive Role of Fantasy in the Fiction of Takahashi Takako." *Journal of the Association of Teachers of Japanese* 28 (1) (April 1994): 29–56.

——. "The Quest for *Jouissance* in Takahashi Takako's Texts." In *The Woman's Hand: Gender and Theory in Japanese Women's Writing*, ed. Paul Gordon Schalow and Janet A. Walker. Stanford: Stanford University Press, 1996, 205–35.

——. "The Liminal Male as Liberatory Figure in Japanese Women's Fiction." *Harvard Journal of Asiatic Studies* 60 (2) (Dec. 2000): 537–94.

——. "The Rhetoric of Reversal in Three Texts of Bliss by Takahashi Takako." *The Journal of the Association for the Interdisciplinary Study of the Arts* 7 (1–2) (Autumn 2001–Spring 2002): 143–70.

Williams, Mark. "Double Vision: Divided Narrative Focus in Takahashi Takako's *Yosōi seyo, waga tamashii yo*." In *Ōe and Beyond: Fiction in Contemporary Japan*, ed. Stephen Snyder and Philip Gabriel. Honolulu: University of Hawaii Press, 1999, 104–29.

NOTE ON EDITIONS

Most of Takahashi Takako's fictional works have appeared in at least two forms. All of the short stories were first published in literary journals, then collected and published in hardcover book editions.

Some of these were later published in paperback book form. Most of the novels were first published as hardcover books and later as paperback editions. In 1989, in compliance with a directive from the religious order to which she belonged, Takahashi had all of her books put out of print. In 1994, *Takahashi Takako's Self-Selected Literary Works* was published. The linked short-story collection, *Lonely Woman*, is in the first volume of this set.

The original publication information for the stories in *Lonely Woman* is as follows:

"Ronrii ūman" (Lonely woman). *Subaru* 16 (June 1974): 148–65.
"Otsuge" (The oracle). *Bungei* 14 (1) (January 1975): 98–119.
"Kitsunebi" (Foxfire). *Subaru* 24 (June 1976): 216–31.
"Tsuribashi" (The suspension bridge). *Bungakkai* 31 (4) (April 1977): 48–67.
"Fushigi na en" (Strange bonds). *Subaru* 28 (April 1977): 46–61.

In 1977 the five stories, collectively titled *Ronrii ūman*, were published together in a hardcover edition by Shūeisha. A paperback edition by Shūeisha appeared in 1982. That book was reprinted several times. The author made minor editorial changes in the stories when preparing them for publication in *Takahashi Takako's Self-Selected Literary Works*. In accordance with her request, I have based my translation on the version that appears therein. This four-volume set contains works of fiction that the author chose and arranged to reflect the development of her spiritual outlook. Because literary excellence was not the sole criterion for selection, some of her most interesting, as well as critically acclaimed, works are not included in the set.